THE LAKELAND
DOCTOR'S DECISION

The Lakeland Doctor's Decision

by

Gill Sanderson

Dales Large Print Books
Long Preston, North Yorkshire,
BD23 4ND, England.

British Library Cataloguing in Publication Data.

Sanderson, Gill
    The Lakeland doctor's decision.

    A catalogue record of this book is
    available from the British Library

    ISBN   978-1-84262-860-7 pbk

Published in Large Print 2011 by arrangement with
Roger Sanderson

Dales Large Print is an imprint of Library Magna Books Ltd.

Printed and bound in Great Britain by
T.J. (International) Ltd., Cornwall, PL28 8RW

Chapter One

One more week, thought Faith as she drove home. She would only be acting head of the Obstetrics and Gynaecology Department at Dale Head Hospital for one more week before the new consultant took over.

Could she bear it? She'd given so much to this department, had taken over so many day-to-day tasks from the retiring consultant Freddie Myers – it was going to be hard to revert to a traditional second-in-command position. What made it worse was that everyone had thought she would get the job. They'd thought it would be a formality. She was Dr Faith Taylor, born and brought up in the area. Dale Head had been her first post after training, she'd grown with the department and knew the hospital inside out. She was quietly – and justifiably – proud of the changes in practice she had made over the years, the department now ran so much more smoothly.

But the Board had ignored all this and had appointed someone else, a high-flyer from a large Birmingham hospital, with a wider history of surgery and – crucially – experience in running his own, much larger, department.

Boards prefer to appoint from outside. They think it shakes people out of a rut. Those had been Freddie's apologetic words when he'd broken it to her that she hadn't got the promotion. To Faith it had been like a kick in the teeth. She loved Dale Head Hospital, but she felt it had betrayed her. Perhaps she *had* been stuck in a rut for too long. Perhaps it was time to move on. Certainly she wouldn't have anything like her current freedom and responsibility under a new, high-flying consultant who was intent on making the department his own.

Enough of work problems. As always, she felt a lightening in her heart as she turned into her drive. When she and Mike were house hunting and they found Fell View cottage in Little Allaby, they had fallen in love with it on sight. A grey stone building with a thick slated roof. A hundred and fifty years old at least. It looked sturdy, made to last.

People often asked if she felt lonely now, living on her own. Well, if she was going to feel lonely then this would be the place she'd pick. But she wasn't. She had her memories, her two younger sisters lived only five miles away in the family home, she was happy in the village, and she loved her job. It was all the life she needed. Loneliness wasn't a problem.

But she *was* tired. She picked up the mail from behind the door and went upstairs to change out of her formal suit into shorts and a t-shirt.

She'd worked a full day and a fair bit of the previous night, but it was still only six o'clock. She decided to take a mug of tea into her garden and enjoy the evening air. As she waited for the kettle to boil she leafed through the mail. So much of it was junk, thrown unopened into the waste paper bin. A couple of bills and... She frowned, recognising the handwriting on the next envelope. Why should her retiring consultant be writing to her? He was supposed to be enjoying the last few days of his holiday, playing golf with an old friend on the other side of the Pennines. She slit the envelope open. There were several sheets of typed A4 inside, along with a handwritten note on hospital paper.

Dear Faith, I've persuaded Tommy to send these details and an application form to you before the post is officially advertised. Give you time to think. Go for it. I believe you would stand a good chance. Freddie.

What was this all about? What post? She knew Freddie had very much wanted her to succeed him as head of department – but the job wasn't his to give. She took her tea and the details out onto her patio. As she read the information, she felt a small knot of ... excitement? Apprehension? It seemed the present Obs & Gynie department head at Hadrian's Wall hospital – Freddie's friend Tommy – was also retiring. Applications were invited from suitably qualified candidates to begin work next January. There followed a description of the job and a list of the qualities required.

Faith knew the hospital, had helped out there several times and liked it. She found herself agreeing that she stood a very good chance of getting the post. It would be better than hanging around here, humiliated at being passed over. She felt challenged – and also disturbed. Perhaps it was the thought of having to make a new start, of leaving where she was comfortable.

Ridiculous, she said to herself. She knew in her heart this was what she must do. If things had worked out as they were supposed to, she and Mike would have been happy in Little

10

Allaby, would have raised a family, would have settled even further into the village. Any progress in her career would have taken place at Dale Head hospital and it wouldn't have mattered when. But things had not worked out that way. Mike was gone, there was no family, and Faith had her future to think of. She certainly wasn't going to put herself through the pain of a relationship again – the only thing left was her professional life.

Boards prefer to appoint from outside.

In Faith's job she was used to making split-second decisions. She made one now. She pushed the tea to one side, fetched a pen, filled in the form. No need to look anything up, she had all the necessary details in her head. She stuck a stamp firmly in the corner of the envelope and strode up the side path to the post box before she could change her mind.

Then she walked back and made herself another mug of tea. She'd done it. Taken the first step. She closed her eyes, telling herself it was for the best, trying to relax.

The sounds of home soothed her. There was the faint hum of occasional traffic, the chirping of birds in her little cluster of trees, the distant sound of someone's radio playing, and ... that was unusual. From somewhere quite close came the sound of a child murmuring as if talking to herself or maybe to a toy. Faith had largely brought up her two younger sisters, she knew an imaginary game when she heard one. But who could it be? There were no children nearby that she knew of.

She opened her eyes, looked down the length of her garden. Her garden backed onto another one, belonging to a cottage similar to hers. It had been vacant for quite a while. There had been interest in it but the price was too high for most locals. She wondered if had been sold at last.

Faith stood and walked down her garden. 'Hello,' she called. 'Anyone there?' She didn't like mysteries involving children.

She noticed her shed door was open. It had a habit of not latching properly. As she reached out her hand to shut it, there was the sound of a giggle and a stern 'Shh, Panda.'

Faith realised there was a gap at the end of her boundary fence. If you were small it would be possible to squeeze through from that garden into hers. From there a little girl could sneak up behind the bushes and into the garden shed. She grinned. 'Coming to get you! Ready or not!' This was a game she had played with her sisters. There was another giggle – an excited one.

She crept round the back of the shed, popped her head around the open door. 'Found you!'

In a corner of the shed, a mischievous expression on her face, sat a little girl in a red dress. She carried a slightly grubby, bright pink panda by one arm. At the sight of Faith she shrieked with laughter.

What was she doing here? She was about five years old, perhaps a few months older. Her body and face still had the chubbiness of childhood but Faith suspected that in time this little one would be a beauty. Flying dark hair, the most wonderful green eyes. Her expression was odd. Faith was good at reading faces, she thought it a necessary part of a doctor's skills. And although she was laughing now, there was unhappiness in the back of those lovely eyes.

'Hello,' she said. 'My name is Faith. This is a surprise, finding you in my shed.'

'I'm Molly. Me and Panda are 'splorers.'

'That's exciting. Where have you explored from?'

'Our new house. We were thirsty and there's nothing to drink 'cos I drank all the orange and there's no water in the tap and

Daddy says we can't go and buy something till this man comes, so Panda and I...'

'Molly! Where are you? Oh heavens, Molly! Molly, come here! Now!'

It must be Molly's father. Faith could hear the panic in his voice. She darted out of the shed. He sounded close.

'Molly!' Yes, the voice was coming from the next door garden and sounded absolutely frantic.

'Over here,' called Faith at once. 'There's a little girl in a red dress playing hide and seek in my shed.'

'Oh, thank God!' The man raced up his lawn, placed a hand on the fence to test it for steadiness, then vaulted over with no further ado. Faith was impressed, he was an athlete!

She went back into the shed. 'I think Daddy is worried about you.' She held out her hand but Molly lifted her arms to be picked up. Faith did so.

The man pelted into view, catching himself on the open doorway. 'Molly! I was so worried. You know better than to run away. What have I always told you?'

Molly's arms tightened round Faith's neck – and Faith found herself liking it. 'Me and Panda wanted to 'splore.'

14

'Then explore with me, sweetheart.' He held out his arms and Molly reached for him, wrapping her arms round his neck as tightly as they had been wrapped round Faith's. The man brushed the hair from her eyes, kissed her on the forehead. 'No running off and hiding, remember? It's not a good idea.'

He looked at Faith. 'Hi. I'm sorry about this but at times Molly...'

Good voice, Faith registered. Low and musical and friendly. The kind of voice that made you feel comfortable, feel wanted. Then for the first time she looked closely at him – and blinked. Where had this man come from? He was big, broad-shouldered, trim-waisted, his body looked toned. His brown hair was curly, the sort that looked just as sexy crisp as it did dishevelled. He was dressed casually, in chinos and black t-shirt, revealing muscular arms. Faith was impressed. This was a really attractive man. But as he had a family it was a good thing she wasn't interested in men any more.

His eyes met Faith's in an equally startled fashion. After looking at her for just a little longer than he might have, he glanced down at his daughter. 'Molly, what am I going to do with you?' He looked up again. 'I'm so sorry

15

if she disturbed you. She's new to gardens. She was probably excited.' He scrubbed his hair with his free hand. 'And she likes hiding. It worries the living daylights out of me at times. How did she get here?'

Faith shook herself free of those eyes. They were also a glorious shade of green, the same as his daughter's. 'There's a gap … one of the fence panels…'

'I'll see to it.'

'You?'

He took a deep breath. 'We're moving in, as you've probably guessed. It's taking longer than I expected and unfortunately we've run out of anything to drink. There's supposed to be a man coming to turn on the gas, water and so on and I daren't leave the house till he shows up. I can't find the stopcock. I was looking for it when I realised Molly had slipped away.'

This was Little Allaby. People hung together, people helped each other. And this chap was clearly approaching the end of his tether. Faith smiled. 'I can't tell you where the stopcock is – every cottage's plumbing is unique along here – but would Molly like to stay and have a drink of orange with me now that she's found her way here? I know you don't know me but we could sit out on my patio up there so you can see us from your house all the time while you go back and wait, it might keep her amused.'

'Want orange!' shouted Molly. 'Want to sit on the pat ... patio.'

Faith was surprised. Why was the child shouting all of a sudden?

'You don't mind?' The man looked at her, startled. 'Molly can be a little – demanding.'

'I don't mind at all. I brought up two younger sisters. They're adults now, of course, but I well remember what they were like. I can handle it.'

'Want orange,' Molly shouted again, obviously feeling that there was no need for extra conversation.

'Molly! Try to be nice for a minute.' His expression suggested that he didn't think Molly being nice for a minute was very likely. But she had been a sweetie when playing in the shed. What was going on?

'It's no problem, really.'

He hesitated. 'No, we'd better go back.'

He was obviously cautious about leaving his child with someone he had never met before. Faith liked him for it. She said, 'I know what you're thinking, but once you've lived here for a while you'll know that Little Allaby people are genuinely public spirited.

Molly and I will be on the patio, sitting in the sun. You'll never not be able to see her, I promise. If she gets to be a handful I'll bring her back, otherwise collect her when you're ready. If it's Jack Kirk who's going to help with the house then you can bet he'll be on time. He's very dependable.'

'I think the name I was given was Jack Kirk. Look, you're very kind, but–' He paused, wincing as Molly wriggled to the ground. 'All right,' he said as she opened her mouth and drew breath to yell again. 'You can stay. Will you be good for the lady?'

'She's called Faith. And she's going to get me some orange.' Molly smiled sunnily up at her father.

Then the man smiled, really smiled, and Faith was lost. It showed him as he should be, a loving father relieved that his child was happy.

When he turned that same smile on her, Faith could see he was genuinely grateful. How could such a warm, smiling man have such an awkward daughter?

Ignoring the strange ripple that ran through her, Faith said, 'I hear the sound of rattling that can only be Jack's van. You'd better go. Come across when you've finished.' She reached out and took the little girl, who

18

promptly grabbed her hand tightly. It was obvious that she had no intention of letting her new friend go just yet.

The man smiled again and said, 'I'll see you in a few minutes then. Faith is a lovely name, by the way.' Then he turned to lope down her garden and vault the fence again.

'Carry me,' said Molly. Faith was happy to. There was not much weight and she was a strong person. So why was her heart beating so quickly? Holding Molly's small, warm body firmly, she walked back to the house.

It struck her that she hadn't asked her new neighbour's name, hadn't asked anything about him. Then again, there had hardly been time. She could rectify that when he came back for Molly. She realised with a nasty jolt that she was attracted to him. Physically attracted! That would never do. His wife was presumably inside, sorting out the cottage, assuming Molly was safe under her father's eye. Faith hoped when she met her that they'd get on. It would be tricky if not.

Once on the patio she sat Molly down and told her she was to stay right there and she would fetch some orange. 'Not orange with bits in,' said Molly. 'I don't like bits.'

'No bits,' Faith promised.

'And I'm hungry. Daddy gave me a sandwich but I didn't like it. He didn't cut the crusts off like Grandma does.'

Faith paused, puzzled. 'Grandma makes your sandwiches?'

'When I live there. But now me and Daddy are going to live here.' Faith felt that she was getting more information than was proper. 'What kind of sandwiches do you like?' she asked briskly.

'No crusts. And I like white cheese that you spread and green crunchy circles on it.'

'I'll do you a sandwich like that. But I'm going to eat your crusts. My grandma always said crusts would make my hair curl.'

Solemnly Molly looked at Faith's dark bob. 'You haven't got curly hair. It didn't work did it?'

'It doesn't work every time, but I keep trying. You sit here in the sun and I'll be back in a moment. Remember we promised Daddy he would always be able to see you.' Faith went into her kitchen to pour the orange and make a sandwich, looking out of the window at Molly all the time. It was a good thing she'd stopped at the bakery on her way home and bought a wholemeal loaf.

After finishing the drink and sandwich Molly investigated the top of the garden asking the names of plants and flowers and wanting to know if any fairies lived here like they did in her books. Faith made sure that she was always clearly visible from the other house. She noticed that although she was chatting happily, Molly constantly looked at the end of garden. Eventually she asked. 'When will Daddy come to get me?'

'I think it'll be very soon,' said Faith, hearing the rattle of a departing van, and two minutes later they saw him walking down his garden. Molly ran to meet him, arms waving. Faith walked down too, smiling at him.

'You were right. It was Jack Kirk,' he said. 'That man is a miracle worker. He went straight to the stopcock – in the coal shed of all places – turned on everything, told me to avoid the wasps' nest in the wall, said he had painted the house four years ago and the paint was good for another ten. I'm going to enjoy living here.' Once again, so easily, he vaulted over the fence. 'Thank you so much for looking after Molly. I'll take her now and not bother you any further.'

'Want to stay in Faith's garden,' Molly screamed and clung to Faith's leg.

Hmm, a bit of a change in temperament

there. Faith looked at the rising colour in Molly's face and said hastily, 'Would you like a cup of tea? We're going to be neighbours after all.'

He hesitated, glancing at his daughter. 'If you don't mind, I'd love one. I'm Chris, by the way. I forgot to say.'

'I was impressed by the way you leapt over the fence. Are you a gymnast?'

He smiled. 'Far from it, but I spend time in the gym when I can. It tires me and relaxes me at the same time. Not that I usually need tiring.'

That smile again! Faith felt amazingly warmed by it. Also perturbed. 'Come up to the house. Molly has had a sandwich, I hope you don't mind. Would you like one?'

'I don't want to put you out. I brought provisions with me. And you've been very good when you don't even know us.'

'You'll get your chance at being good back,' she said. 'That's how the village works.'

'Then yes, I'd love a bite to eat.'

'For filling, I've got some local ham.'

'Wonderful. When we get settled you must tell me the best shops.'

She went into the kitchen, quickly assembled a tray. Why was she going to all this trouble? Because they were going to be neighbours, she told herself. That was all.

She sighed. *No*, she thought honestly. She was attracted to this man. That was not a good idea for all sorts of reasons. It was also a startling one. She *never* felt this way about casual acquaintances. She needed to sort out her reactions and then be a bit more distant.

She carried the tray out onto the patio, liking the way he stood up as she approached. He was standing quite close to her. For a moment she saw a look in his eyes that she recognised – and suspected that her eyes were transmitting the same message. Chris was as attracted to her as she was to him. Oh dear. Now what?

She poured the tea, gestured for him to help himself from the plate of sandwiches. Molly slid off her seat to go exploring down the garden.

'Has she been okay?' he asked.

'Yes, no trouble at all. Though she did start getting anxious about you.'

He rubbed the back of his neck. 'Look, I wouldn't normally say anything, but as we are going to be neighbours and you'll probably see quite a bit of Molly in the garden, I think it's important that you understand about her. I'm telling you because I don't

23

want you blaming her for the way she acts sometimes, especially if she's noisy. It's really not her fault.'

Whatever was he going to say? Faith wasn't at all sure she wanted to know but, 'Go on,' she said. How could she not if Chris felt it had to be said, despite it hurting him. And he was hurting. Faith could tell.

He took a quick breath. 'Molly's mother and I are divorced. After Molly was born Lorraine suffered from baby blues – it's not uncommon. But things got worse and slowly she lapsed into full clinical depression. I was desperate. I did everything I could, but it got so that she hated me and blamed me for the state she was in. In the end I had to accept what the doctors said – that alone, she would be able to pull herself out of it the way she wanted to. She simply didn't want me around. So we parted and I kept Molly. But it hasn't been easy for any of us. Molly got really messed up by it all.'

This was something Faith had come across before. Post-natal depression of that intensity was very rare, and always tragic. But it happened. 'And you still feel guilty?' she guessed.

'Yes, of course. About both Molly and Lorraine.' Then, in a different tone, 'This is wonderful bread. You must tell me where to buy it.'

Fair enough, Faith thought. He's confided what the neighbourhood needs to know and doesn't want to go any further. Was he warning her off? Had he felt that he and she might be...

But now it was his turn to be curious. 'Do you live here on your own?'

It was a graceful way of putting it. She nodded. 'I've got my work and that is enough to keep me happy. No man in my life.'

The atmosphere changed infinitesimally. 'But there was one once?'

There wasn't any need for her to be as free with her history as he had been with his. 'I'm always busy. I'm a career woman. I've got male friends, plenty of them. But no one in particular.'

'Daddy! Come and look! What is it?'

Chris smiled at her, raised his eyebrows. 'When do children stop asking questions?'

She grinned. 'Never. It's just that as they get older it's called scientific curiosity.'

She watched as he walked over to Molly and hunkered down with her to examine one of the rose bushes. He walks well, she thought. He's at ease in his body. She felt a

25

flutter of apprehension. Less than an hour since she had met him for the first time – yet each minute made him seem more and more attractive. But they'd only just met! There was so much about him that she didn't know. And she didn't want – or need – a man!

He walked back, holding his daughter's hand.

'It was a ladybird and it moved,' the little girl said, enchanted. 'It was red with black spots. I've seen them in pictures, but I didn't know they were real! Daddy told me what to say. "Ladybird, ladybird, fly away home. Your house is on fire, your children are gone." And it did fly away.'

'I should think so too,' said Faith.

Chris didn't sit down. 'We've bothered you enough,' he said. 'It's been lovely to meet you and to think that Molly and I have made our first friend here in Little Allaby, but now I have to get her bathed and there's a fair amount of arranging to do. And a lot of stuff coming up later.'

'Of course. Have you got a job nearby?'

'Quite close, yes. I've just taken a post at Dale Head hospital. I'm going to be the new Obstetrics and Gynaecology consultant there. I start work next week.'

Faith felt herself blench. Her head reeled as she grappled with what he had just said. This couldn't be happening! The man who had got her job was living next door! And she liked him. It was all too much. She clutched at the arms of her chair for support.

Chris saw her shock. 'Are you all right, Faith?' he asked, obviously concerned. 'You've gone pale.'

'I'm fine, fine,' she gasped. 'You are Mr Ford?'

'Yes, but how did you...?'

Faith knew her voice was too high, but she couldn't get it down to normal. 'It's an interesting coincidence, you being a neighbour. I'm your Senior Registrar.' She forced her hands to loosen, laid them in her lap. 'We're going to be working together.'

And that was going to be very, very hard.

Chris sighed as he leaned over the bath, dripped in the favourite bubble mixture, whirled the water round with his hand. Bedtime with Molly was often a trial. In fact, life with Molly was often a trial. He loved her more than he could say, he understood her problems, he'd even consulted a child psychologist for advice about her behaviour.

He might be an expert in O & G, but he wasn't too proud to ask for help when it was needed.

The child psychologist in Birmingham had said what he had already worked out. 'Chris, there's no great worry. And no medical treatment needed either. She'll grow out of these tantrums. You know – everybody knows – that you've done everything possible for Molly and Lorraine over the past few years. But Molly has seen the deterioration in Lorraine, must have overheard arguments, furious rows, not known how to react when Lorraine was in one of her silent phases. And yes, your parents looking after her while you worked was obviously the most sensible thing to do – but they've gone overboard making it up to her and she's got spoilt. So now Molly is taking it out on you. The bottom line is that she is scared that you too might move out of her life. What she needs is to be able to feel confident in your love, to feel certain that you won't abandon her. That might take some time. Until she does feel confident, she'll behave badly by the polite world's standards. It's the only way she knows of getting your full attention.'

'I'm going to see she gets all the attention she needs,' vowed Chris. 'My new post will be less stressful, that's why I took it. And it won't take up so much of my off-duty time. Molly will be my life.'

The child psychiatrist coughed. 'I'm glad to hear it. There's just one thing more. Be careful not to form any ... any fresh relationship so that Molly feels left out. That would only make things worse.'

Chris thought about this now as he called for his daughter and a little naked girl ran into the bathroom. He lifted her up, slowly slid her into the water. 'Do you like your new bedroom, sweetheart?' he asked. 'We can paint it any colour you like.'

'Pink. I want pink. Faith is nice. Can I go there again?'

'We must be careful not to bother her. She's a hard-working lady and...' He saw the lower lip begin to quiver. 'I'm sure we can see her now and again.' He wondered if Faith would be as happy about that as Molly. His daughter might have been no trouble today, but she could be very demanding.

Molly settled down to enjoy her bath. He had wondered if she might be overtired after the long car journey from Birmingham, but for once there were no bedtime tantrums, no crying and not letting him leave her bedroom. He had thought she was bound to

29

be upset at this huge change. But surprisingly she was not. Either the novelty or more fresh air than she was used to this evening must have affected her.

He read her a story – well, all right, two stories – then kissed her forehead and held her hand. And then she was asleep. Looking at the small angelic face, Chris felt a surge of love. There wasn't anything he would not do for his daughter. She'd been messed up so much already. For the time being he had to devote his life to her. He turned on the child alarm and went downstairs.

There was a conservatory at the back of the house. He sat there, a small glass of whisky in his hand and watched the sun go down over the hills. It was lovely. He was going to enjoy living here.

He could look down his garden, see across to Faith's house, and see her lights springing on. For a brand-new acquaintance, she'd been very good with Molly. Probably, he had to admit, a bit better than him. He remembered her saying that she'd brought up younger sisters; that could explain it.

Faith. For a moment he treated himself to the pleasure of just thinking how gorgeous she was. She was a striking woman. She carried herself well, 'walked tall' with ease

30

and grace. She was the kind of woman people would turn to look at as she passed them in the hospital corridor. He wondered what she was like with patients. Brisk? Friendly? Or both? Her figure was nicely rounded, the curves quite obvious in the thin t-shirt she had been wearing. And her long legs seemed to go on forever. Dark hair cut in a short, hospital-efficient bob. When she relaxed her face was beautiful – perfectly heart-shaped with generous lips, dark brown eyes. But Faith – though she'd been calm on the surface – hadn't seemed to relax an awful lot. Several times her expression had been serious, her smile only fleeting. Did everybody have problems? He wondered if he could help at all.

No. Chris shook his head decisively. There was no place in his life for impossible dreams. He had felt an instant attraction to her and knew very well she felt the same. But he had also noticed her backing away when he asked if she had a man in her life. If she had hang-ups about relationships, that would make two of them.

He frowned, swirling the amber liquid in his glass. Living so close, they were bound to see a lot of each other. Molly would want to visit Faith again for sure. Once she took a liking to people, she wanted to see them over and over again. And that being the case, it would be easy for him to get to know Faith. But Chris remembered the child psychologist's warning. He daren't risk Molly's happiness by forming an attachment to Faith, much as the thought tempted him. He would have to keep her at a friendly distance.

Not that he wanted any kind of attachment. After Lorraine ... well he had learned his lesson. He wasn't going though all that guilt, despair and sheer helplessness again.

Another thought intruded – was the distance already there? He had seen the shock in Faith's face when she discovered who he was. He had been jolted himself at the coincidence. But after the shock had come another reaction. She had cooled towards him. Well, he couldn't blame her. A new broom coming into the department, asking questions, making changes. Obviously she would be wary. And a professional distance was the best thing possible to begin with. It would make it easier for him too.

But there was that physical attraction... No!

One thing, one principle was laid down, hard as granite wherever you worked. No patient would suffer because of staff's personal feelings. They had to get on somehow. At the hospital certainly, if not as neighbours. But what was he to do when Molly – as she certainly would – wanted to call on her new friend next door twenty-four hours a day?

Chapter Two

In the end, the problem was shelved for a while. Next morning Chris found a note pushed through his front door. *I'm not around for a bit. Family crisis. Ring Jack Kirk if you need to know anything. The other neighbours are all very helpful too! Love to Molly. Faith.*

It was thoughtful of her to let him know. She must have called very early, before he was up. He wondered if this was on purpose. That she didn't want to see him again until they had established a working relationship. He didn't consider that she might have posted the note the night before.

Later in the morning he took Molly for a walk through the village. He had only cast a rapid glance around when he'd dashed up to view properties, but now came to appreciate it. They called at the Post Office with its attached shop and he was pleasantly surprised at the quality of food that was for sale. He walked Molly past the primary school she would be attending, then, hearing the cheerful shouts of children in the playground, they doubled back and went in to arrange an induction day. Then they stood on the bridge and looked down at the river bubbling below them. 'Ducks!' shouted Molly. 'Daddy, look, ducks! Can we go down and paddle and give them some bread? Look, there are some people there doing it.'

'Not today, sweetheart, we haven't got any bread. But soon.'

He felt his worries easing. He was going to enjoy living here. It would be simpler to sort out his personal life in a completely new place.

The sun was out, so for lunch they called in at the Earnshaw Arms. He had a pint of bitter watching Molly enjoy herself in the play area. The meal was plain but good, and eating it in the garden added to the treat. This was a new life, he thought, and miraculously Molly was behaving. He only hoped it continued that way.

When he went to pay he chatted to the publican, telling him that he and Molly had just moved into the area.

'Ah,' said the publican. 'Near Dr Taylor, did you say? She's a good doctor. When my daughter was in Dale Head with her first baby, Dr Taylor sorted her out. People think a lot of her round here.' The man looked troubled. 'Poor lass. We were all sorry when...' his voice trailed away.

'Sorry?' Chris asked.

But the man seemed to think he had gone far enough. 'Nothing. I'm sure you'll be happy here. Hope to see you and the little one in again.'

Chris realised that there was something the man was not going to tell him, so didn't try to press it. He would find out in time.

He enjoyed his walk but there was trouble with Molly on the way back. She was tiring and wanted to see her new friend again – and had a small tantrum when Chris told her Faith wasn't at home.

'I can't help it that Faith is at work,' he said. 'She is a doctor in the same hospital where I'm going to be working soon. Doctors are busy people, you know they are.'

Molly's lip quivered. 'Want to *see* her. Show me.'

Chris considered. It wasn't a bad idea. Molly liked to have a picture in her head of where her people were at any given time. It helped to make her feel more secure. And Dale Head had a nursery and a play scheme for staff children for when their parents were working – it was one of the things that had attracted him to the position. With any luck, he could be quite clever here. 'Okay,' he said. 'But you have to be good.'

He was not due to start work at the hospital until next week, but he had always intended to visit for a preliminary look round, maybe a chat with as many of his new staff as possible. This afternoon was as good a time as any for the first visit. He would have to dress a little more professionally though.

'Are we going to see Faith?' Molly asked, submitting to having her face and hands washed and her dress brushed down – where did children acquire so much dust?

'Perhaps,' he said. 'If she isn't with a patient.' He realised he had no idea of her duty schedule or what sort of "family crisis" she might be involved with. Not to worry. Freddie Myers would know. He'd ask him when he got there. At Molly's anxious look

36

he said more firmly, 'I hope so.' Even if he was not exactly sure why. He wanted to see Faith – but he was fairly sure he ought not to.

Work. This was what Faith was good at. She knew exactly what was going on in her department – had all the threads laid out in her mind ready to trace back to the right person should there be a problem. If you worked hard, got engrossed, then there wasn't room in your head for other things. She had worked like this before. When the greatest heartache of all had struck, when she had been devastated by the loss of Mike, her job and her family had helped her through.

First, the morning ward round. Usually she enjoyed this. There were difficulties of course, but it pleased her to see those hopeful mothers whose problems she could deal with. And this had been a good morning – so far.

But now there was a case she could well do without. Ella Greerson. She sighed as she checked the notes, and then pushed open the door of a single-occupancy side ward.

'I know what I want and I'm having it,'

said the girl in the bed. 'It's my decision and you can't stop me. I'm eighteen. I'm an adult. You've got to do what I want.'

Harsh words, but the voice was weak and trembled slightly.

'Good morning Ella,' Faith said calmly. 'We can talk about decisions in a minute. The first thing though is, how are you feeling today? That was quite a scare you gave your employers yesterday.'

'I only fainted! Serve them right, the nosey...' Ella subsided. Her mouth worked. 'Look, I'm feeling sick and I'm fed up with it. I didn't ask to come in. But now I'm here, how about the operation? I just want rid.'

'Let's have a look at you first.'

'I've just been messed about by that nurse! Isn't that enough?'

'We check and double check everyone. Ella, this is something we have to get right.'

'Well, get on with it then.'

Faith knew there was no real anger in Ella, the girl was afraid. Beth Kitson, the senior midwife and duty staff nurse, had gently extracted her story. Ella was young and she was pregnant. She had no partner, the father of her child had disappeared without a forwarding address the minute she had told him she was pregnant. She used to live in Manchester but a year ago had had an argument with her mother, flounced out of the house and left, swearing never to go back. She had come here to the Eden valley, had found a live-in job at a hotel. And got pregnant. Now she was alone and she was scared. Apart from anything else, she would have nowhere to live if she couldn't work.

A quick examination, Faith's murmuring voice explaining what she was doing, the physical fact that someone was caring for her seemed to soothe Ella a little. Faith pulled up a chair to the bedside. 'You already know this, Ella. You're underweight, slightly malnourished and about sixteen weeks pregnant. But your baby is doing fine.'

'Not my baby, I don't want it. I've told everyone, I want rid of it!'

'There's plenty of time yet. We can perform terminations up to twenty-four weeks, if it is really necessary. Usually it happens at about twenty weeks. So there's time for you to think.'

'What's to think about?'

This was the difficult question. How to best help her young patient? Faith wondered if she could find the right words. Ella had to make up her own mind, she could insist on a termination. But it was not an option that any of the medical team here would be happy with. Faith thought of her own family. Perhaps family care was the key.

'Have you any brothers or sisters, Ella?'

The girl frowned. 'What's that to do with anything?'

'I'm just curious.'

'I've got one of each. My sister Mary is seventeen and going to train to be a hairdresser. And my brother Pete is a mechanic.'

'Do you get on with them?'

'We got on all right but they don't know where I am now and I don't want them to!'

'But you miss them?' Faith's voice was quiet.

It took Ella a while to reply. 'I suppose so. A bit.'

'It's good to have family. People who will support you when you're in trouble.'

'I know what you're trying to do, what you're trying to say! You want me to get in touch with them, tell them what a mess I've made of my life. Well, I won't!'

'We can't *make* you do anything. Ella, what do you think your mother would say if she knew that you were pregnant? Pregnant and potentially homeless?'

'She'd go mental! That's why she's not to know.'

'But after she got over the shock? She might even like being a grandmother. When you were young, was she a good mother to you?'

'Yes,' Ella said after the longest of pauses. 'She was good while we were all young. We were all happy then. Till my dad wandered off.'

'Right.' Faith stood. 'I've got to move along now, Ella, but if you ever want to talk to me – just ask. I want you to stay in another night for observation. Is it okay if I ask one of our counsellors to come along and speak to you?'

'Will she try to talk me out of getting rid of the baby?'

'No one's going to talk you out of anything. She'll tell you your options. What Social Services can do. What it's like caring for a baby on your own. You're not going to be abandoned whatever you decide.'

Another long pause. Then, in an apparently casual voice, Ella asked, 'What would you do if you were me?'

'It'd be hard,' said Faith, taking the girl's hand, 'but I'd phone my mother. Just to hear what she had to say.'

'I'll think about it,' said Ella.

I'm a doctor, not a counsellor, thought Faith

as she walked down the corridor. *But I hope I got that right.* Once she had so much looked forward to being pregnant herself. Once. To deal with someone who was considering throwing that away was hard.

Time for a snatched roll and coffee at her desk while she caught up with the never-ending paperwork. She was just thinking she might be making some headway with it when there was a knock at her door. She glanced up as the door opened and there was Chris! And looking even better than he had yesterday. All the problems she had pushed to one side when he'd left her garden rushed back to engulf her without warning.

'Is this a bad time? Are you busy?' he asked.

'Very,' she said, struggling to keep her voice professional. 'I'm always busy. But come in and sit down.'

He came and sat opposite her. He had no right to be there looking so wholly gorgeous! In fact, he shouldn't be here at all. He wasn't starting until next week. Faith needed time to organise her feelings. She resented this sense of being harried.

'How is the family crisis?' he asked. 'Hopefully not too bad if you're working?'

'No, not too bad after all.' Up until this

moment, Faith had been feeling a bit foolish about the way she had overreacted last night. Now she wasn't so sure. 'My sister Hope had got herself into a state over her latest boyfriend,' she said. 'They're always The One – until they aren't. This time it was a particularly messy break-up. Charity and I were needed to administer chocolate and hugs.'

'Faith, Hope and ... Charity?'

She gave him a level look. 'Don't say *anything*.'

Amusement danced in his eyes. 'I wouldn't dream of it.'

'Very wise. We've heard them all before. We've been known to score people on what they say.'

'Ouch. I trust all is well now.'

'For the moment.' Hope was naturally bouncy, unlike Faith. She'd got over this sort of thing before, often. All it had taken was for the three of them to enjoy a giant meal of spaghetti bolognese and a bottle of wine and she was saying she really was giving up men for good this time and devoting herself to her sisters. Faith had gone to sleep in her old bedroom wondering where she'd heard that before.

'Good.' Then Chris's face fell. 'Boyfriend

trouble – I suppose I've got all that to come with Molly.'

'Almost certainly. But not for a long time yet.' Yes, she thought, she had been foolish. This insane instant attraction to Chris had to be dealt with sensibly, the way she approached the rest of her life. Last night she'd been unsettled enough by the encounter with him that Hope's tearful call had been a heaven-sent opportunity to head back to the family home for the night.

'All the same, I'm envious,' said Chris, bringing her back to the present.

'Envious?' said Faith. 'Of what?'

He shrugged noncommittally. 'Of the fact that you have two sisters to share troubles and hugs with. I'm an only child – and a late only child at that. Perhaps if I'd had someone to turn to when things started going wrong for Lorraine, I'd have been better able to support her.'

'You've got friends, surely.' Faith felt a little awkward now.

He gave his lovely smile. 'Lots. But blokes aren't always very good at group hugs and chocolate and deeply meaningful insights.'

'You're lucky,' muttered Faith. Close families could be a mixed blessing. She'd broken the news last night that she'd applied for the

44

post at Hadrian's Wall and her sisters had been suitably encouraging and told her to give it her best shot. But then suddenly this morning Charity had picked up her off-hand comment about having new neighbours at the bottom of the garden and had homed in on it.

'Lucky? What do you mean?' asked Chris, sounding amused.

Faith shook her head. 'Nothing.' And it *was* nothing. Even if her sisters had wormed every last detail out of her about Chris and Molly and had *looked* at each other in that way they had and finally asked what would happen if she got the new job?

'Then I'll let the cottage and he'll have a different neighbour,' Faith had replied.

Charity had shaken her head. 'You fancy him rotten, which hasn't happened since you lost Mike. You don't fall in and out of love at the drop of a hat, Faith. If you like this chap, don't blow it.'

Faith had got up hurriedly. 'Don't be ridiculous. He's going to be my boss. That's the only reason I mentioned him. Because it could be tricky living so close. And he's got the job that should have been mine and that riles me!' And she'd left for work. For heaven's sake, she'd brought them up, advised them through all the angst of adolescence. They weren't supposed to turn the tables and start interfering with *her* life.

But now Chris was here in her room, looking tremendously smart in a dark linen suit and bright blue shirt and giving the lie to her "don't be ridiculous" statement to her sisters.

Well, she was in scrubs. They didn't do much for her, they weren't designed to flatter. But they were a uniform, a sign that she was a worker and that's how people – including him – should view her. She liked wearing scrubs.

'Molly wanted to see where I was going to be working,' Chris told her. 'And where you were working. I wanted to call in any case, I need to make a courtesy visit to Mr Myers.'

'He's away,' said Faith. She knew she sounded abrupt but she would rather have had some warning of his coming. 'Using up the last of his leave.'

Chris looked blank. 'Oh. I hoped he would take me round, introduce me to a few people. Let me get the feel of the place before I start properly. Who's covering for him?'

Faith raised her eyebrows. 'That would be me. I can give you an hour. Where is Molly?'

Chris grinned. She wished he wouldn't, it made him far too attractive. 'We just happened to walk past the playroom,' he said. 'Strangely enough she wanted to go in and play. She was quite happy for me to leave her there for a while.'

'Handy,' said Faith dryly. 'Especially as she'll probably spend quite some time there this summer while you are working.'

'It's certainly a relief,' admitted Chris. 'And it's partly what attracted me to the hospital. But I wouldn't have left her if I hadn't been happy. However, it looked secure and well staffed and the lady in charge – Abbey, I think – seemed very competent. Molly took to her at once, thank goodness. It doesn't always happen.'

'Abbey is lovely,' said Faith. 'She's a tie with the village, as it happens. She's Jack Kirk's wife. I know her quite well.'

How ironic. Faith didn't tell Chris that it had been she who had proposed the playroom, had pushed for funding to be found for it, had suggested Abbey Kirk as the nurse in charge. It was more than a playroom. It was also a nursery and a crèche with twenty-four hour coverage. Staff found it a huge help to have somewhere they could leave their children and know they were safe. Thinking of the good she had done the hospital, she felt upset again. Chris's job should have been hers!

There was silence for a moment as he looked at her and she felt warmth creeping up her body. Her heart was beating faster than usual, her breathing faster and more shallow. What was wrong with her? These were the classic signs of ... never mind what they were the classic signs of.

She seemed to have completely run out of small talk. All she was aware of was that he was there and he was looking at her. She stood, knocked over papers on her desk and bent down in confusion to pick them up. Then she realised that her unflattering scrubs fell forward as she did so – to hug her figure and show the outline of her underwear. Hastily she straightened herself, but noticed his eyes were on her bare arms and neck.

He cleared his throat. 'I suppose you think I should have phoned ahead,' he said, sounding less polished than earlier.

'It might have been more convenient,' muttered Faith, 'was there anything special you wanted?'

'Several things. But first, this might seem a bit ridiculous but might I bring Molly here for five minutes? It's just that she'll feel happier knowing where you are. Then I can take her straight back to the playroom and we can have a brief chat.'

'If she wants to, of course.' Faith thought it an odd request, but she'd rather like to see the little girl again. Chris nodded and left the room.

His being away gave her time to get her reeling thoughts in order. She was not a callow girl, shaken by the presence of a handsome man, she was a respected senior registrar. She did not faint over the best looking man she had come across in years. *No?* a little voice asked. No, she muttered to herself.

He returned with Molly, sat opposite her with his daughter on his knee. That smile was devastating! It made her want to do anything for him, just so he would smile at her. Then she wondered. Did he smile like that at everyone? Was it just a carefully practised tactic? It seemed genuine, but how could she tell?

'Hello, Molly,' Faith said. 'It's nice to see you again. How was your first night in your new house?'

Molly considered a moment. 'The birds waked me up,' she said, 'so I had to go and

49

get in bed with Daddy.'

'And then you woke Daddy?'

Molly giggled. 'He didn't mind.' She looked round the room. 'Are those story books?'

'No, sorry. I need them to help me with my job. Do you like reading?'

'Daddy reads to me at bedtime. I can read some of the words, but I like pictures best. If you come to my house, I can show you.'

'That would be very nice.' But Faith wondered about going to Chris's house. Did she want to? Did she want Chris to drop in at her house like other neighbours did? Chris wasn't like other neighbours.

Chris seemed to be having similar thoughts. He picked up his daughter. 'Come on, sweetheart. You've seen Faith's room, now it's time to get back to the playgroup so I can have a proper talk to her about the work we'll be doing. Wave goodbye.'

'Bye, Faith.' Molly said, waving. 'See you soon.'

Faith only managed to type up a couple of sentences before Chris was back.

'Thank you for letting me bring Molly,' he said. 'Now she can fix you in her mind, she knows where you are. And that is a comfort to her.'

'I'm happy to help, she's a lovely little girl. What did you want to talk about?' Faith kept her voice professional. She hoped it was about work, she could hold her own there.

To her surprise a shadow crossed Chris's face. 'I *should* be discussing how we are going to work together. Obs & Gynie is my job and I take the smooth running of my department seriously. But it's Molly I want to ask you about first.'

Oh no. This was going to be difficult. Faith liked the little girl and felt sorry for the way her young life had been messed with. But she did *not* want to be drawn into too close an intimacy with Molly's father. Sinfully attractive or not, he still had her job. And it had given her a painful jolt when he'd said the words *my department*. She looked at him. Although she was trying to remain calm, she suspected he somehow knew what she was feeling. Why wouldn't her heart stop beating so fast? Much more of this and she'd have to take a pill to calm down. Then she realised this was silly.

Chris looked away, almost as if he was embarrassed. He *was* embarrassed, she realised. He didn't like to admit that he needed help with his own daughter. Faith's heart melted – but only for the little girl! She resolved to find out what he wanted.

But he was glancing round her room, putting off the moment. She knew it was like her, a reflection of her personality. She kept it absolutely neat and tidy, wanted as little fuss as possible. She could put her hand on any record or reference within seconds. She was not like other people who filled their room and workstation with pictures, post cards, personal memorabilia. The room was almost aseptic – which was what she wanted.

There were just two photographs. One was of herself and her sisters. The other was of her parents. Chris picked them up.

'I can see the resemblance,' he said. 'You're a handsome family.'

Handsome? Was that some kind of compliment? She supposed so. 'Thank you,' she said.

'And these are your parents?' A picture of Mum and Dad in an African clearing, surrounded by a crowd of grinning children.

'Yes. That was taken in Kenya, three years ago. It's one of their more presentable photos. At the moment they're in Crete, running a clinic in the hills. They spend a lot of their time abroad, helping wherever it's needed. They always have.'

'And left their children at home? Was that why you brought your sisters up?'

Faith flushed. This man was too bright. Had he detected a faint touch of resentment in her voice? Quickly she said, 'They are committed to what they do. We weren't abandoned. We had Dad's cousin living with us, but because she was much more interested in her thesis than the real world, I took over. It worked okay.'

'I still envy you.'

It wasn't just a courteous statement, he meant what he had just said. He did envy her closeness to her family. *I'm an only child.* Faith met his eyes, aware of a sudden intimacy. They had both revealed something of their inner selves. For a moment it brought them dangerously close.

It was Chris who recaptured the conversation. 'Anyway, back to my problem. Molly is starting at Little Allaby school in September, and I'm hoping she'll be happy in the playroom here at the hospital until then. But there are bound to be times when my working hours don't coincide with her "home" time. Do you know someone in the village who provides reliable childcare? Someone you would personally vouch for?

I've let Molly down enough, one way and another. I can't have just anyone looking after her.'

'A live-in nanny?' Faith suggested.

'I thought of that, it's the obvious thing. But it's not what I want in my home. Molly is my child. She comes first with me and I want to come first with her. I don't want her to have a sort of surrogate mother.'

Faith warmed to him when he said this, he was obviously sincere. But she thought there was a touch of a warning there too. Chris was not going to be diverted from what he saw as the most important thing in his life – diverted by a relationship with a woman, for example. A woman such as herself. Well, that suited her fine. In fact, it was a relief.

'Shouldn't be a problem,' she said more briskly than she intended. 'I believe a minibus goes round the local schools bringing children to the play scheme here for the after-school session. The crèche is open all night with a skeleton staff. Or if you prefer it, with Abbey Kirk living in the village, you won't be short of a sitter in the evenings if you need one. If not Abbey, then there will be other people she can recommend.'

'That sounds good. Thank you. So have

you got time to show me around the O & G section? Just a quick, informal visit? I'd like to have someone with me so I don't have to introduce myself. Of course, if you've got other things to do...'

'I've always got things to do,' she said, 'but yes, there's time before my clinic.' And then she couldn't help herself. She cleared her throat. 'Quite a lot of the ... arrangements here have been my suggestions. But you might have your own way of doing things.'

For a moment she caught a glimpse of Chris the professional. The man who cared about his work. 'I'll not alter anything that is working well, no matter who arranged it. If I think anything has to be changed – then it will be – though after consultation.' Then he smiled that smile at her and said, 'but I'll bet there's not a thing you arranged that I want to interfere with.'

Why did she get such a glow from that little compliment? 'Let's go then,' she said.

They walked through the hospital corridors, Faith noticing the turned heads and curious expressions. Who was this handsome stranger? They'd find out soon enough. A couple of times they passed senior figures in other departments, and she introduced Chris to them. This should be Freddie's job. As so often before, Faith was doing it for him.

Chris said, 'As soon as I start properly I'd like to call a couple of department meetings and meet as many of the staff as possible. I want to tell them the kind of work I expect and what they can expect from me. Then over the next few weeks I'll talk to everybody individually. They need to know that we are a team, that everyone's work is important, from the consultant to the ward clerk. I believe in the personal touch.'

'Sounds good,' said Faith reluctantly. Despite herself, she was impressed by his enthusiasm and sincerity. How different he was from the retiring head of department. Freddie Myers was old school, he believed in a rigid medical hierarchy with him firmly at the top. She was the only person in the department entitled to call him Freddie. And that only when they were alone. For the rest of the time, or the rest of the department, it was Mr Myers or sir.

They arrived at the door of the Delivery Suite, the place where much of her work was carried out. Faith tapped in the code to unlock it. Once inside they both rinsed their hands with the alcohol rub. Clean hands were all important here. Then along the corridor for a white coat each.

This was Faith's empire and she felt it wrap itself around her, soothing her. She walked past Reception, the assessment area, the equipment room, the High Dependency rooms, the theatre and the wards. She nodded and smiled at the staff she knew so well. They greeted her, openly curious about the tall man by her side.

As they walked, her eyes skimmed everywhere. She needed to be certain that all was as it should be. It generally was. She had excellent staff. But she felt a pang. They were not her staff any more. They were to be Chris's. She doubted that he would give her as much responsibility as Freddie had. Her step faltered. She had enjoyed that responsibility.

Protocol indicated that they call in to see the staff nurse on duty. Beth Kitson smiled as Faith pushed open her door. 'No problems here, important person. We're all happy and settled and ... oh!'

Faith knew what had happened, knew even without the disturbance in the air that had caused her white coat to brush her legs. Chris had entered the room behind her and Beth had seen him, presumably for the first time. Faith could hardly fault her friend's reaction. Chris was an impressive man. For a moment Faith had a worrying vision of what it was going to be like to have a young, sexually attractive man as head of a department that was very largely staffed by women. And when they found out he was single, it could cause havoc!

She took a deep breath. The staff would take their tone from her. Another reason to be cool and clinical. 'I'd like you to meet Mr Ford, the new consultant and head of department,' she said. 'Mr Ford, this is Staff Nurse Beth Kitson. She's our most experienced midwife and is going to be one of your right hands.'

'Mr Ford?' Beth's welcoming smile died. 'I'm pleased to meet you, sir.'

Faith didn't dare look at Chris, but he must have felt the suddenly chilly atmosphere. Beth was her friend, of course, and had been furious when Faith had been passed over for head of department. But still...

'I'm looking forward to working with you, Beth,' said Chris with a smile. 'I've not officially started yet, and this is your section. Do you mind if I tag along with Faith here and look round a bit?'

He was good, Faith thought. What's more, the request had been sincere. Technically a midwife was in charge of the room where a birth was taking place. Only when the midwife asked was a doctor allowed to take over. And Beth was both midwife and staff nurse.

So Chris was recognising Beth's importance and Faith saw that Beth appreciated it. 'You're very welcome,' she said, a small blush on her cheeks. 'I'll be here if you want to come back to ask any questions.'

Faith led Chris round, showing him the key areas, introducing him to the staff on duty. Everywhere they went, people grew cool as soon as they learned who Chris was. He couldn't fail to notice. Faith could sense him working extra hard to deploy that smile to show he was approachable.

After a while he said, 'This hospital is so different from my last one. It's quite startling. The friendliness, above all. You seem to know most of the staff here really well.'

Faith hadn't really thought about it like that. But it was true. 'Yes, I suppose I do,' she said.

He was silent as they paced along the corridor back to her room. She wondered what he was thinking. 'I really must get back to my paperwork.'

'And I must collect Molly.' He looked at her, a crease on his forehead and his glorious green eyes sombre. 'Faith, thanks for putting up with me this afternoon, but I get the feeling that there's lot to be worked out between us.'

'I don't think so. Not when we are both concerned with the good of the department.'

Chris shook his head. 'I'm learning that this hospital is vastly different from the one I was in before. It isn't a workplace, it's a family. Families are partisan. And they also feud.'

'I think you're exaggerating,' she said. 'I'm sorry, I must dash.'

He put his hand on her arm. 'I'm not having feuding in my department. I need to talk to you, but on neutral ground. When are you coming back to Little Allaby?'

Talk? What sort of talk? She moistened her lips. 'I was only away for the night. My sister lives on an emotional roller-coaster. She's back to normal now.'

'Then would you come round and have supper with me after work? I'd suggest taking you out for a meal but there's no way I can leave Molly. Come after she's gone to bed. If she knows you're downstairs she'll play up.'

She met his eyes, trying to ignore the colour and the way the wry question in them made her heart beat faster. 'Is my coming round to your house a good idea?' She didn't say why it might not be so clever and she was glad that he didn't ask. But they both knew why. There was something between them, something that made the air crackle when they got too close. That was something else that had to be sorted out.

'For the moment I can't think of a better one,' he said. 'You do agree that we have to talk?'

She thought of the way her department had closed ranks against him, warming her with their loyalty even as they'd embarrassed her. He deserved an explanation. 'Yes, I suppose I do.'

What was happening to her? She was used to medical emergencies, staff problems, administrative disputes – and she knew they had to be dealt with calmly. There was never any point getting agitated over them, it was always counter-productive. Clear, calm logic was her way. That was why she had thought she was so good at running the department. But now she felt her pulse racing. She hadn't been so moved by proximity to a man since Mike had last... No, she wasn't going to think of Mike now. She was over it.

Her way meant dealing with problems

head on. Working with Chris, she sensed, would be different. That smile of his made you lose sight of grievances for a start. So, yes, she would meet him away from this department which she felt was hers and he was determined would be his. She looked at him. He was intent, now. Perhaps troubled too.

'So you'll come?' he asked.

'Yes, okay. Say nine o'clock? But just for a coffee. No food and no alcohol. I'm on call tonight.'

'As you wish. I think that we...'

Nothing was ever certain in an Obs and Gynie department. They were just about to let themselves out when there was an anxious call from behind them. 'Faith! Mr Ford! Wait!'

They turned, there was Beth moving rapidly towards them, concern on her face. She reached them before she spoke, you don't shout medical details down corridors. 'We've got an emergency. Birth seemed to be going fine, midwife quite happy, no trouble, but now – there's a prolapsed cord.'

Instantly Chris's demeanour changed. He became alert in a second, hurrying alongside Faith as she strode back. 'What are you going to do?'

'Examine the patient. Perform an emergency Caesarean if necessary.'

He nodded. 'I'll observe. Be your second.'

Faith was shocked. He hadn't even started work here yet! She would have preferred to have her junior registrar as second. But for the good of the department and the sake of working with him in the future, there was nothing she could say.

Chapter Three

'I've sent for the anaesthetist and the paediatrician,' Beth said. 'The theatre will be ready as soon as you are.'

Faith nodded. She knew how speedy and efficient Beth was. She ran through the details in her head. A prolapsed cord. The membranes had ruptured and the umbilical cord had slipped below the presenting part of the baby. The baby must be stopped from being born, it could lead to its baby's early death. There was no way of foretelling a prolapsed cord, sometimes, fortunately rarely, it just happened.

Rapidly, they walked into the delivery

room and Faith took in the details at once. The mother on her hands and knees on the delivery couch, the midwife – an older, experienced nurse, using her fingers to carefully hold the presenting part of the head away from the cord.

Chris whispered to her. 'Quick examination then you go and scrub up first. I'll talk to the mother and the father, explain things and try to calm them a little.'

'Good idea,' Faith said, just a bit miffed at not thinking of this herself.

As she made her lightning examination she heard Chris say to the panicking mother, 'It's Mary isn't it? Well, Mary, we have a bit of a problem here but we think we can deal with it. Your baby doesn't want to be born in the usual way so you're going to need a caesarean section. Try not to worry, okay? We'll have you in the theatre in a couple of minutes.'

It was his voice that did it. It was calm, confident, relaxing. Faith watched the worry on the parents' faces easing, then left and went to the theatre scrub room.

After a moment Chris joined her, began to scrub up himself. The anaesthetist was dealing with Mary, they had a couple of minutes to themselves.

'Sorry I jumped in, but I like to be familiar with the skills of my staff and this seems a good opportunity for me to observe you.'

Faith's lips tightened. Freddie had done little staff assessment recently – what *had* been done had been done by her. Oddly, this was even more cause for irritation.

Chris persisted. 'Do you have any objections to my being here?'

Yes, she did have objections! She didn't want to be observed, perhaps criticised, by the man who had taken her job. *She* should have been the one observing. The logical part of her mind told her that this was not an unreasonable suggestion. But her professional pride wasn't always logical and she would also liked to have been asked first! 'You're the head of department,' she said crisply, 'or you will be soon. It's not for me to have objections. Now let's get this baby born.'

Chris looked at her thoughtfully. 'Faith, you are lead in this operation. Unless you ask me to, I'll do nothing but watch, just forget I am here. Of course, if you want any suggestions...'

Her voice was cold. 'I feel quite capable of performing this operation. I have performed it before.'

He ignored the chill in her voice, though she was sure he had recognised it. Instead he smiled. 'And now you are thinking that whatever happens, you will never ask for my advice.'

Who did he think he was! She shook her head crossly. 'That would be sheer stupidity. You are half right. I desperately want not to have you assist me. But if it is necessary for the patient's well-being, then I will ask for help without a second thought.'

His smile disappeared, to be replaced by a look of what she could only think was respect. 'Faith, I was making fun of you and you gave me the perfect professional response. This is a serious time and I am sorry for my juvenile words.'

Damn the man! It had been a gracious apology. Now she had no reason to dislike him.

'Let's get started,' she said.

Now she was scrubbed, gowned, masked. Her patient was wheeled in, lifted onto the table. Faith looked at the woman's abdomen, surrounded by green sheets. She glanced around: anaesthetist, scrub nurse, Chris by her side, waiting for her lead. The paediatrician waited. The moment the baby was born it would be handed over, no longer Faith's concern. Her concern would be solely the mother. All was prepared.

As ever, she took the few seconds she always gave herself before the first cut. Three deep breaths. And then began.

Sometimes it was surprising how little time an operation took. Faith cut down carefully, reached in and then – there was the magic moment when they heard the baby's first tiny cry. The paediatrician took her – it was a little girl – and Faith continued with the delivery of the placenta. She looked at Chris. 'Would you like to close?' she asked. After all, if he was observing her, why couldn't she observe him?

'If you don't mind.' Chris stepped forward, bent over the patient. Of course he was masked, there was no way she could see if he was smiling. But his eyes crinkled slightly and she knew he had guessed what she had been thinking.

She watched him, hands deft as he sutured. And she had to admit it to herself. He was good!

He finished, they nodded at each other. The patient was taken to recovery, for the moment she was the anaesthetist's responsibility. In time she would be taken down to the ward where they would see her again.

There was that feeling of satisfaction as they both stripped off their scrubs, threw them into the bin.

Faith looked at Chris. 'Did I pass?'

He sighed. 'You're not going to let me off easily, are you? Yes, of course you passed – not that it was an exam. You knew you would, otherwise you wouldn't be a senior registrar. And I'll offer a bit extra, your skill with a scalpel goes beyond mere competence, it was superlative. I'm lucky having someone like you on my team.'

It was a generous response and she felt ashamed of her waspishness even if the words *my team* rankled. There was something she knew she had to say, although it hurt a little. 'I liked working with you too. We're a ... we're a good team.'

'So we are. Faith, I was already pretty certain that you'd be a more than competent surgeon. But now I've observed you, I'm completely sure. Don't make this hard. Isn't it a fair thing for a team leader to try to find out?'

'Yes,' she said. 'Yes, naturally it is.' She didn't say that if she had been a team leader, she'd have wanted to watch the work of a new second in command. But she felt it. And was unsettled because of it.

He looked at his watch. 'About our meeting tonight...'

'It's all right,' she interrupted. 'It's not necessary. There won't be any more trouble with the staff, Chris.'

And there wouldn't. She would go round tomorrow telling her people not to give him a hard time. Yes, this was her department, but he was doing exactly what she would have done in his place. She couldn't fault him for that. When she left, she would leave knowing Dale Head O&G was in a safe pair of hands.

'But I wanted to...'

He was looking at her, puzzled. She managed a bright smile. 'Shoo,' she said. 'Go and find Molly, she'll be wondering where you are. We'll be neighbours at home and colleagues here. It'll be fine. It'll be for the best.'

He made a small helpless gesture, the sort that said men simply didn't understand women. Then he disappeared.

Chris had collected Molly and had gone home. Faith still had several hours work to do. As always, she found immersion in the business side of the department stopped her thinking of – of things that worried her.

Mysteriously, when it *was* time to leave, she dallied. She visited the patients, had a coffee with the ward staff, knew she was wasting time. Why did she not want to go home? Fell View cottage had always been her haven, her refuge. But now it held Chris at the other end of the garden. She didn't want to think about him. He attracted her, and that frightened her. She was never again going to put her heart in anyone else's power. It hurt too much when they dropped it.

Come on, she told herself. *Face up to the problem! Move!* She did. She glanced inside the playroom on her way towards the main door. Just one night nurse and a couple of children, cuddled up next to her watching a video, waiting for their parents. As always, Faith's heart twanged, imagining for one stupid moment that they were her children, that she'd go in and say she was done for the day and they'd all go home to the cottage. *Stop it. That way madness lies.* Faith turned sharply away, and as she did so, caught a flash of bright pink from the Wendy house. She frowned. Was that...? She looked closer. It was. There could be no mistake. A slightly grubby bright pink bear with a black head and one floppy arm stared up at her from the floor. Molly had left Panda behind.

Faith looked at the toy, dismayed. For all she knew the child had dozens of toys and wouldn't miss this one until next week, but ... but she remembered her sister Hope at that age, dragging Bunny round with her, and the tantrums whenever Bunny got himself unaccountably lost just before bed-time. Visions of Molly, waking in the night, distraught, flooded Faith's mind. She would have to take Panda back.

She keyed in the pass code and opened the door. The nurse looked around. Faith scooped up Panda. 'This is Molly Ford's, isn't it? I'd better drop it in on my way home.'

The girl nodded and made an okay gesture. Because after all, it was the obvious thing to do.

Faith had never been in the cottage at the bottom of her garden before. It had belonged an old gentleman who didn't encourage visitors. After he died she had seen painters renovating it. Presumably Chris had been over the place and decided to take it one time while she had been at work.

She couldn't vault the fence at the bottom

of her garden, as Chris had done. Probably she could have scrambled over or squeezed through the gap in the fence, but she decided to walk round to his front door. It would be more formal.

What it would be like inside? It was a traditional Lakeland cottage like hers. It would be difficult for it to be too dissimilar – the difference would be in the personal touches. Then again, he'd only just moved in. She realised she was deliberately concentrating on the house so she didn't have to think about Chris.

When he opened the door she got a shock. Again. Could you get used to having a shock? Wasn't a shock supposed to happen just once? Whatever, seeing Chris in front of her – even though he'd been in her operating theatre that afternoon – gave her the now familiar feeling in her throat and chest, almost a lack of breath, a stirring of the heart. This was crazy. She had to get used to this man. How were they to work together for the next six months otherwise?

He must have smartened up to visit the hospital, because he was now dressed as he had been when she first met him. Chinos and a dark t-shirt. She couldn't help admiring the flatness of his waist, the muscles in his arms.

He smiled, surprised to see her – and that raised her temperature even higher. *I'll bet he smiles on purpose because he knows the effect it has*, she thought, striving to be detached.

'Hi,' he said. 'This is unexpected.'

'I'm not staying. I thought Molly might want...'

His eyes dropped to the toy tucked under her arm. 'Panda!' he said in tones of utmost relief 'Oh, Faith, you life-saver! Where was it?'

'In the hospital playroom. I saw this flash of pink by the Wendy house as I was leaving just now and thought I should investigate.'

'I am so glad you did. That deserves a drink at least. Come in.'

'No, I...'

'You're on call, I remember. Tea, then. Please? The kettle's just boiled.'

It was the *please* that did it. 'Not for long, then,' she said, stepping inside. 'I've only just got back.'

He frowned. 'That's late.'

'You know paperwork. If you don't do it, it mounts up.'

He rubbed his chin. 'And I stopped you doing it when I called?'

Faith flushed. She hadn't meant to sound critical.

'Are we understaffed?' said Chris abruptly. 'I know doctors are used to working long hours but if you'll forgive me, you look tired out.'

'The department works fine,' said Faith, bristling. 'I've been covering for Freddie, that's why there's more bookwork than usual.' It was high time to change the subject. 'Where shall I put Panda? I hope Molly found another toy to cuddle.'

'Several,' said Chris over his shoulder as he headed down a hall the twin of hers. 'I got her off to sleep eventually but only with four stories and her other soft toys tucked up in bed too. We looked everywhere for the blessed thing.'

'I used to have to do that with my sister Hope's rabbit. It was the most miserable-looking thing, but Hope has always been a soft touch for waifs and strays. She's got a heart like melted butter. Jumble sales adored her because she'd buy up all the leftover cuddlies at the end.'

Chris grinned. 'And does she still?'

'No, she collects unsuitable men instead. Starts each love affair with boundless energy, and then weeps all over us when he cuts and runs.' She regarded Panda. 'Anyway, this reminded me of Bunny. The same mournful expression and floppy arm from being dragged around.'

'You got it. The trouble is, we haven't been here long enough for Molly to identify favourite hiding places. She likes small enclosed spaces that she can see out of.'

Faith smiled. 'Like sheds.' She remembered where she'd seen Panda. 'And Wendy houses?'

'Exactly. "Open-womb" I call it. Come in. Sorry about the mess. This place is nothing like a home yet. There's a lot still to do.'

He ushered her into the lounge towards a coffee table and two couches. She looked round and saw what he meant. Had she wanted to see personal touches? There weren't any. No pictures on the wall. No ornaments. Just a row of books along the floor: Daddy's and Molly's side by side. Faith felt a strange lump in her throat.

'I'll get the tea.' He walked into a back room that – if it was like her own cottage – must be the kitchen, returning with two mugs and a pile of sandwiches on a plate. 'I was making these anyway,' he said. 'Please help yourself.'

About to demur, Faith realised she was hungry. She stretched towards the plate and was surprised into a laugh at the neatly cut triangles. 'I can certainly tell you're a surgeon. It looks as if you used a scalpel to cut the sandwiches. All exactly correct.'

'I hate shoddy cutting,' he said with a grin that did strange things to her pulse rate. 'Now, eat and drink, with my thanks for Panda.'

'It was nothing.'

There was an awkward pause. 'Faith, is it going to be a problem? Me being your boss at the hospital and living here next door to you?'

This would be the time to say *No, because I hope to be leaving in six months anyway*. She hesitated. It would seem awfully rude if she did that. 'It's not the situation I would have chosen,' she said carefully. 'It's not a good idea to have work overlapping into home life.'

She bit into a precise triangle of seed-strewn brown bread filled with what she realised was a local cheese. He'd wasted no time in finding the best neighbourhood shops. 'You make a good sandwich.'

The first slightly bitter expression she'd seen crossed his face. 'Over the past few years I've done a lot of catering for myself. I decided some time ago that if I had to live on sandwiches, then I might as well make them good ones. Faith, you might not want to mix your two worlds, but there's one puzzle I need the answer to before I do anything else.'

'I'm listening.' She wasn't going to offer anything until she found out where the conversation was going.

'When I was being shown round I could have made ice cubes with the atmosphere every time you introduced me as the new head of department.'

Faith bit quickly into another sandwich. 'Really?' she mumbled.

'Now, I know new faces always bring some suspicion but this was more than that. And being a bright chap, I think I know why. Would I be wrong in guessing that a number of people thought *you* were the proper person for the job? That there is a feeling in the department about it being unfair that an outsider had beaten you to the post?'

'I ... I applied for the position, of course...'

His eyes met hers, serious and concerned but with a hint of steel in their green depths. 'Let me say straight away that I can completely understand the attitude. You appear to be both competent and popular. But we need to clear the air right from the start. Do you feel the same way? That you were unfairly cheated out of a job?'

Faith leaned back in the chair, took a breath. She had never backed down from a fight but she arranged her words carefully before she spoke. 'The Board is entitled to appoint who they like. And the word cheated is wrong, I'm sure they made their decision honestly. But yes – I feel ... I feel disappointed. I've always been absolutely loyal to Freddie, but I've been working towards the job for the past few years. I suppose you could say I felt I deserved it.'

'I appreciate your honesty. Is it going to stop us working together?'

She shook her head decisively. 'No. Certainly not. I have never let personal considerations get in the way of the efficient running of the department. Patients' welfare must come first. And I know already that you want the best from your department, just as I would. That's why I said earlier that there wouldn't be a problem. Because I'm going to go round tomorrow and sing your praises.'

He nodded. 'Thank you. I appreciate it. Do you...' He broke off, listening.

Faith blinked. What was that noise ... the place wasn't haunted, where did the whimper come from? She saw Chris close his eyes briefly, and in that moment he looked tired to death. The whimper came again, then a full outburst of crying. Faith realised what it was, a baby alarm. Molly was waking up.

Chris stood and picked up the pink bear. 'I'm sorry. With any luck the sight of Panda will soothe her. She is still insecure at night,' he said. 'Once, Lorraine went out and left her – I didn't realise until I got home after a late shift and found Molly hunched up in the alcove under the stairs bawling her eyes out. She's getting better now. Sometimes it only takes five minutes and she goes back to sleep.'

'It's not going happen this time,' Faith said, listening to the increasing strength of the cries. 'You'd better go up. I'll see myself out.'

But then there was a series of thumps, the crying changed in tone, and with a hurtle of feet, into the room burst a small, blue-pyjamaed figure. 'Daddy, I didn't know where I was and Panda is lost and I'm thirsty and I thought you'd gone and...'

Chris swept the flushed, tear-streaked child up into his arms and rocked her. 'There, sweetheart, it's all right now. I was only down here. I promised you I wouldn't leave, remember? That's why I took you with me to the hospital earlier. And look who decided to stay there because it was such a nice place.'

'Panda!' yelled Molly, hugging the pink toy as if she'd never let it go.

'Yes, so we'll go back upstairs and I'll make your bed again and...'

Faith stood. She'd been about to leave anyway, and now she was doubly in the way. Chris would have his hands full with his daughter for some time. But Molly turned her head and saw her.

'Faith,' she screamed, 'I want Faith! Daddy, I want Faith to hold me.' She held her arms out still clutching Panda, kicking and flailing so wildly she was likely to unbalance them both. Faith saw the look of desperation on Chris's face.

'Shh,' he said. 'Faith's got to...'

'No!' Molly screamed louder.

Faith didn't want to get involved, but no woman on earth could have walked away from those heartrending sobs.

'Want to hug,' gulped the little girl, and made a renewed effort to scramble across. 'And I'm thirsty.'

Chris sighed. 'Just for a moment, then, while I get you a drink.' In an instant Molly's hot damp cheek was against Faith's and she felt the weight of the small body in her arms.

80

'Want milk,' said the muffled voice. 'Warm milk.'

'Milk's no good for quenching a thirst,' said Faith, sitting on the couch with Molly on her lap burrowing into her chest. 'Water's much better. Dear me, you have got yourself into a state.'

She couldn't read Chris's expression as he looked at the two of them. He turned to get the water without comment.

Faith held the heaving little body close to hers, felt the strength of the sobs slowly diminish, felt the tears running down Molly's cheeks dry up. She was not sure of her feelings. She hadn't wanted to get involved, but there was satisfaction in calming the little girl. And something else. A tiny tug of something missing from her life.

Chris came back with the water. Molly was persuaded to sit between them on the couch and drink it. She wanted both Faith's and her father's arms round her as she pretended to give Panda a drink. Faith was in a short sleeved shirt, Chris was in a t-shirt. Both had naked arms, their bare skin touched and she could feel his warmth. It was only a touch but pleasure stirred inside her and she wondered if she should get so much enjoyment from something so simple.

She tried to move her arm, Molly pulled it back. Chris looked at her over Molly's head and shrugged. Faith would have preferred it if he could have smiled a little. Surely he could see that she hadn't asked for this to happen?

It only took another few minutes, Molly really was tired. The beaker slipped in her hand and her eyes started to close. She leaned against Faith as her father removed the drink, fetched a flannel and gently wiped her tear-streaked face. 'Do you mind coming up to her room?' he asked in an undertone. 'Just in case she has another tantrum.'

'Okay.' She followed as he carried Molly upstairs, swiftly pulled the child's bedclothes together and watched while he laid her down and tucked her in amongst her fluffy toys. When he kissed her forehead, something deep in her heart stirred.

'She's asleep,' whispered Chris. Still he watched until Faith made a movement towards the door. He gave himself a little shake. 'Sorry,' he said, following her out to the landing. 'She's had such a rough time this past year. And we've moved from pillar to post until I'm not surprised she doesn't know where she is. I'm hoping we will set up a stable home life here. Thanks for your help, Faith. Quickest I've settled her back for ages.'

'Only too happy,' she said. 'I'd better go now.'

'Yes, of course.' He paused with his hand on the door latch. 'Why did you say water, not milk? Not that I'm ungrateful, because usually she makes all sorts of fuss about it being too hot or too cold and not being like Grandma's and...'

Faith grinned. 'That's why. It takes five days to break a habit, but only one to make it. She didn't really want a drink at all. Just your attention. Plain water at night means she doesn't have you running around trying to satisfy her, you are still in control, and it's not sufficiently exciting to make her want to repeat the experience tomorrow.'

Chris rubbed his jaw ruefully. 'I told you my parents spoilt her. That was another reason I wanted to get us away. Thank you again. I'd see you home but ...'

'But Molly is upstairs and my front door is only a three minute walk from yours, so don't be silly. This is Little Allaby, not some great restless city. Good night, Chris. I hope the rest of it is undisturbed.'

'I could do with a decent night's sleep, that's for sure,' He released the door handle and his arm brushed hers.

Faith wasn't a touchy-feely person. She certainly wasn't an indiscriminate hugger and kisser. Sisters and parents, yes, but very few others. She kept a certain reserve. But now, perhaps because of the sigh in those last words, perhaps because of the drawn look in his eyes whenever he mentioned Molly, perhaps because she still felt a bit guilty over the way her staff had made their partisanship known, she gave Chris's forearm an awkward squeeze.

He stilled, looked down at her. The faint touch of citrus aftershave came down to her, warmed by the scent of his skin. A warm, exciting, essentially male combination.

It would take so little, thought Faith, shaken right out of her comfort zone. Just tip her head upwards a tiny bit. That's all it would need. The temptation was there.

She stepped back. Inside she was yearning, and she was terrified. Something was telling her that everything would be all right, that this instant attraction was okay. Something else was telling her not to be a fool. That she was letting an attractive man and his vulnerable daughter make merry with her emotions.

No. Not again. It wasn't going to happen.

'I have to go,' she said, trying to get the words out evenly. 'I'll see you when you start properly next week.'

'Yes...' Chris's lovely green eyes were dazed. Had he felt it too? That tug?

'Sleep well,' she said, and left.

Chris stood in the darkness and watched Faith walk away. I could have kissed her, he thought, the way she looked up at me, the way she tilted her head a little, I could have kissed her. I think she would have liked me to kiss her and I ... I half wanted to.

No! He turned away from the window. First, most important, he had Molly to think of. Second, it would be foolish to start any kind of affair with someone he would have to work with. And third ... the third reason was the memory of Lorraine. The horror of the past few years was still with him. He couldn't risk going through anything like that again.

Faith was not for him.

Chapter Four

Faith walked round to her own cottage not knowing what to think. That had been too close. Much too close. How on earth was she going to work with this man for the next six months? Could she blame it on tiredness? She'd had a hard day – like all days recently – and she needed peace. She had always thought of herself as a determined person, if there were problems in her life she would face them and deal with them. But this situation was different. And she didn't like it.

The next day she kept her word to him. As she did her rounds, she let it be known that she was pleased with the new consultant. In the departmental staff room she mentioned how much Chris had impressed her. For a hot-shot city doctor, she added, not wanting to appear so full of praise that people started wondering why. But every word she said added to the feeling of guilt that she should have let the partisan feeling build up in the first place. It didn't make her feel any better when mid-afternoon she took a call that had been routed from Freddie's phone and a sultry voice asked for Mr Ford.

'Mr Ford doesn't start work until next week,' said Faith crisply. 'This extension still belongs to Mr Myers.'

'Oh.' The voice sounded disconcerted and considerably less sultry. 'Are you sure? Mr Ford was in a finance meeting this morning. I've got the figures he wanted.'

It was news to Faith that Chris had come into the hospital for a meeting, but then why would he tell her? She'd only been running the department in Freddie's absence. What's more, she had now identified the voice on the phone. Veronica Beresford from the bursar's office. Divorced, predatory ... it was a sign of things to come. Her irritation grew.

'Thanks. If you send the figures through the internal mail, the O&G secretary will see Mr Ford gets them next week.'

She put the phone down and pressed her fingers to her temple. Just for once she decided she would leave work on time. She called her junior registrar, told him he was in charge, and went home to get some much-needed peace in her garden.

At home she did half-an-hour's gardening and then sat on the terrace with a mug of tea just watching the green horizon of the Pennines. She was deliberately not thinking about work or neighbours or decisions. And then the peace was broken by sound of a child's angry screams.

'I want to see Faith! I want to see Faith! I want to see Faith!'

It was Molly, bursting out of her own cottage, her little legs pumping down the next-door garden path.

'And I said no, Molly.' That was Chris, running out after his daughter. 'Faith is a busy doctor. She might not even be at home. Even if she is, you can't just burst in and see her like that. It's very rude.'

'She IS home. I can see her.'

'Molly, stop it.' Chris caught up and lifted the little girl into his arms.

Molly's screams rose. 'Put me down. Want to see Faith. I hate you!'

Faith stood up and strolled down to the fence. 'Goodness me, what a noise,' she said mildly.

'Faith!' Molly wriggled and stretched out her arms.

Chris held on tight. He looked fraught and embarrassed. 'Sorry. I asked her to play quietly by herself while I made a phone call and...'

Faith held Molly's tear-filled gaze. 'Daddy is quite right,' she said. 'You can't just run into someone else's garden as if it was your own. But if you stop crying and ask nicely, you can play here while Daddy makes his phone call.'

Molly gulped back a sob. 'Can Panda come?' she said in a small voice.

Faith nodded.

Molly slithered down and trotted back to the house.

'You don't have to do this,' said Chris. 'I wouldn't normally let her get away with a tantrum but an old friend has just had bad news about his wife's illness and I...'

He looked tired to death. Faith's heart twanged. 'Shh. Of course you must ring him. Molly will be okay with me.'

'Thank you. I know she will. I don't understand. I thought she was settling down. She's been so good today. She went to the playroom this morning while I was introduced to the joys of the hospital budget. Then we made lunch and had a nice walk around the village. And now she's suddenly a monster again.'

'Jealous?' suggested Faith. 'Because you

wanted to do something at home without her?'

'Maybe. The child psychologist I consulted suggested that Molly misbehaves because she's frightened that I might leave her like her mother did. She needs all my attention – emotionally, anyway. She mustn't see me getting too friendly with anyone who might take me away from her.' He made a frustrated gesture, his face bleak. 'So I say I need to make a phone call and she shouts out that she hates me.'

Molly reappeared with the familiar pink toy. Faith put her hand on Chris's arm, needing to make him feel better. 'She didn't mean it. She doesn't really hate you. Children always dare most where they feel most safe. My sisters used to save their very worst language for me, but the good news is that they grew out of it once they were in their twenties.'

As she'd intended, Chris gave a small chuckle. 'Their twenties, eh? Nice to know there's a light at the end of the tunnel. Thanks, Faith. I'll come and get her when I've finished the call.'

'No hurry,' said Faith. 'You're allowed to have some time for yourself now and again.' She realised suddenly that her hand was still on his arm and snatched it away just as Molly ran up.

Chris made a show of holding back an overgrown forsythia bush so Molly could get through the gap. Faith got the feeling he was as embarrassed as her at not noticing the prolonged physical contact.

Chris went back to the cottage. It was nice of Faith to cheer him up, but at times like this, with an unhappy task ahead of him, he felt a complete failure. *I hate you!* Those words had cut him to the quick. And yet he *had* to be strong with Molly, he couldn't give in to her every whim as his parents had been doing recently. He had to help his daughter develop into a more balanced little girl.

On his way to the phone, he looked through the window to where Molly and Faith were playing catch, both running, calling, laughing. He blinked, surprised. It seemed to him that Faith was enjoying herself just as much as Molly. She looked so relaxed and happy! No sign of the careful barrier she had erected between herself and him. Just for a moment he caught himself wishing...

No. He set his jaw and pushed the memory of Faith's touch away. He had to remain single in deed as well as in word. He wouldn't deceive his daughter.

Then he thought of his ex-wife and his mood changed. He felt so much guilt for the way he had let Lorraine down. Despite psychologists saying she'd more or less decided in her own mind where to go, he couldn't help blaming himself a bit and was sad at the way things had turned out. He had done everything he could. But it hadn't been enough.

As he remembered dreadful scene after dreadful scene, he shuddered. No way was he going to risk going through that again! Not for Molly or himself. The worry, the heartache, the sleepless nights. He had been burned once, it would be a long time before he would go near that particular fire again.

Fortunately Faith seemed as keen not to progress the relationship as he was. It begged the question of why *she* was so determinedly single. The landlord of the Earnshaw Arms had hinted at something and Chris had sensed a general feeling of sympathy for her during his walks around the village. Every time he'd mentioned her name there had been a wave of warm regret. He wondered who had hurt her and why. No, he didn't simply wonder – he felt angry with whoever had hurt Faith.

Faith and Molly played in the garden for a little while, then went into the house. Faith had forgotten how tiring small children could be. Molly had a little girl's curiosity and wandered round happily. She opened cupboards in the living room, peered inside the fridge in the kitchen, washed her hands in the bathroom. Most of all she loved Faith's bedroom.

It was a simple room, white walls with just a touch of pink, built-in pine furniture, a dark rose carpet contrasting with a pink throw on the bed. There was a view of the hills from the window. Faith had positioned the double bed so that in the morning she could look out at the line of green peaks. It was the room she and Mike had been going to use, but...

She sat down abruptly on the bed trying to hide her sudden tumultuous thoughts. Was it having Molly here? Reminding her that she was now alone? But she had accepted that! Yes, she and Mike had spent time planning and decorating. A partnership, they had agreed on so many things. And then he had died. And she had felt her heart die with him and made her decision never

ever to put herself through that pain again.

Now she looked at the pictures she had painted – one wall covered with paintings of landscapes, paintings of family, simple paintings of flowers. How long was it since she had had a brush in her hands? Not since she had heard about Mike.

'Who drawed all these, Faith?' asked Molly, fascinated by the paintings.

'I did, sweetheart. I used to paint a lot.'

Molly stared at a picture of the fells. 'I like drawing,' she said. Faith stood silent, thoughtful for a moment. Then she took a deep breath and made a decision. After all, how hard could it be? 'Well, let's go down to the kitchen and perhaps we could both do some drawing.'

She sat Molly down at the table and gave her an orange juice. When she was much younger she had loved painting with her sisters. But now she would help Molly to crayon, not to paint. Using water-colour paints with a little girl was fun but it frequently involved spattered clothes which would then have to be washed at once. Not something she wanted to wish on Chris. Perhaps some time she might tell him to dress Molly in a paint-acceptable outfit so they could... No, don't plan!

She slipped into the back-scullery to fetch paper and crayons. All her art material had been stored here. Her paints, brushes, easel and everything else, all neatly packed. She remembered the tears as she cleaned everything, wrapped it, put it away. It had been like saying goodbye to an old friend – but the urge, the need, even the ability to paint, had vanished. She hadn't been sure it would ever come back.

'What are you going to draw? Something for Daddy?'

'Ladybirds,' Molly said after a moment's thought. Her eyes widened. 'Did you know there are some in our garden too?'

She sounded so surprised that Faith laughed. 'The whole world is one big garden to insects. They just pick where they want to go. Draw one first and then colour it in.'

Molly concentrated, bent low over the paper and drew a thick, wobbly red circle. Faith looked at her bowed head and couldn't help a feeling of loss, of chances now gone. Chances gone for good.

It seemed no time at all before Chris was politely tapping on the back door. Molly slid down from her chair, good as gold and happy to see him. Chris met Faith's eyes with a helpless shrug.

'Are we all going to have tea here again?' Molly wanted to know.

'Not today, darling,' said Chris. 'That was just special for our first day.'

'Oh, I forgot,' said Faith as she saw them out. 'You had a call this afternoon from Veronica Beresford in the bursar's office. Something about some figures. I told her to put them in the internal mail.' She carefully didn't ask what the finances referred to, though she would have liked to know.

'Thanks,' said Chris. 'That was efficient. I told her there was no hurry. I want to play with the costs to see if we can squeeze an extra member of staff out of the budget.'

Somehow Faith didn't think it was playing with *costs* that Veronica had had in mind. But she kept the thought to herself.

She felt strangely restless once they'd gone. She picked up Molly's discarded crayons, sketched a ladybird herself. Hmm, not very good at all, she needed to practise. She sketched another one. Yes, this was better. There was a vague yearning inside her, making her uncomfortable. Dammit, this was Chris's fault. Chris and Molly. She'd been perfectly content before they moved in next door. Now she was having to remind herself daily that she was never going to get involved with

96

a man again – and she was having wistful thoughts about painting!

All right. She'd accepted that she should be moving on. That's why she'd applied for the job at Hadrian's Wall hospital. If she got it she would be head of her own department. Lots of work, lots of responsibility, she would revel in it.

Or was it something other than work that she needed?

The traitorous thought was in her head before she could keep it out.

'No!' she said in distress. 'No!'

She whirled back to the scullery with Molly's crayons. And stopped, deliberately conjuring up memories, deliberately reminding herself of the pain that love could unknowingly bring.

There was a mural in here. She'd wanted to bring the garden into the house, so she'd painted flowerbeds and trees around the walls. Mike had loved it. He had appreciated her work so much, more so because he couldn't paint himself. He had thought being able to draw and paint was wonderful. Sometimes he used to lean over her shoulders as she worked. And then he'd gently ease her hair aside and kiss her softly on the back of her neck. 'Mike, I can't concentrate when you do that,' she'd said, mock-reproachfully.

'So do you want me to stop?'

'Just once more,' she would say. 'Or perhaps twice. But it's nice and it makes me want to...'

Once, as a joke, when she was sketching in the garden, she had given him a pencil and asked him to draw the front of their cottage. He had tried and the result had been terrible. Then she had picked up the pencil and had altered what he had drawn – and made it quite a reasonable picture. He had been delighted! 'We're a creative couple,' he had yelled. 'Just think how beautiful our children will be! Perhaps we could go and...' But they had had no children.

When he had died, she had tried to paint. When they were together it used to calm her, bring her peace. But painting brought back memories of him that were too painful, so she had stopped. Completely. Stored all her art material and wondered if she would ever take it out again.

'Now do you remember?' she demanded of herself aloud. 'Do you remember the desolation? Remember the emptiness? That's why you're not falling in love again. Not ever.'

She put the crayons away with a slam of the cupboard door and in doing so the next door swung open. Charcoal sticks. Faith looked at them. Charcoal wasn't painting. It wasn't colour. And her hand, mysteriously, was aching to draw.

Okay then. She sat at the kitchen table where Molly had sat, stretched out the first sheet of paper, rolled the charcoal rod between her fingers. No flowers. No trees. Nothing to remind her of Mike. She found herself sketching Molly's face, trying to show the eagerness, the happiness as well as the childish beauty. She could feel what she wanted to draw but it somehow didn't come out quite right on the paper. She tried again. This time profile rather than full face. And Molly grew on the page, just as she'd wanted. Faith felt her heart expand, felt her eyes fill. It was like riding a bike, or going home to supper with her sisters. Something you didn't forget after all.

Who to draw next? Chris kept coming into her mind. But he would be harder. It wasn't just a question of lines and shade; a good drawing of a face told you something about the feelings you had for the model. She knew what she felt about Molly but she was not so sure about Chris. He had an interesting face, she'd like to draw him sometime but first she needed to get her thoughts in order. At the moment her emotions regarding him were confused. They altered from day to day – even from hour to hour.

She looked at the sketch of Molly. She wasn't as expert as she used to be. But the excitement was returning. Perhaps this was part of pulling herself out of her long period of mourning. Something that would help her face up to starting a new life.

With a flash of understanding she realised that this was partly down to meeting Chris. That moment the other night, that exchange of glances, that awareness – had made her realise how wrong it was to lock up feelings. Locked up feelings are liable to break out at the most awkward moments!

So maybe she would do one more picture of Molly – in the garden shed, perhaps, with that mixture of mischief and excitement on her face – and then she would sketch Chris after all. It would show her subconscious that there was nothing to be alarmed over. It would get him out of her system.

Molly was happy. Chris had to admit that playing with Faith had been good for her. She was very proud of her drawing, it was fixed to the fridge with one of the fairy magnets Grandma had given her. He realised that she was tired but not over-tired. Bathing her and putting her to bed was comparatively peaceful and she was soon asleep. Faith had worked out just the right amount of excitement a little girl should have before going to bed. Chris didn't know whether to be irritated or grateful. Why did she not have children of her own? The thought came uninvited: she would make a good mother.

He sat down at the table and looked unenthusiastically at the notes he had made in this morning's finance meeting. He should get a head start on his new job by going over the previous budgets – but that image of Faith laughing and darting about the garden with Molly was getting in the way. No! This was ridiculous. Work, that's what was required. He bent his head to the notes.

'I don't quite see,' said Chris pleasantly, 'why there was so much less budget available to the O&G department last year.'

Veronica Beresford smiled sympathetically at him. Today she was wearing a dark blue dress that did wonders for her figure, even if she had decked herself out in a little too much jewellery for his taste. She looked sorrowful at his question. 'There was a Project,' she said, her voice husky. 'I'll show you.' And she swept him off into the corridor before he realised what was happening.

'You could just tell me,' began Chris, but Veronica had her arm through his and was hurrying him down the stairs from the bursar's office.

For a moment there was a flash of real feeling in her face as she said, 'I argued against it – told them it was unnecessary but no one agreed. All that money! Quite ridiculous.'

They were heading for the main corridor. Chris wrinkled his brow, trying to think what there was along here to put the bursar's assistant in a passion. A familiar figure, tall and easy-striding, turned the far corner coming towards them. Faith! Chris was horribly aware of Veronica's arm through his and tried to disengage it, but the woman hung on.

'There,' she said, stopping dramatically. 'This is the culprit.'

They had halted outside the playroom. Chris blinked, not understanding.

'Back so soon?' said Faith, pausing beside them. 'You'll be charging overtime in advance.'

'Mr Ford wanted to know why his new department had so little budget,' said Veronica. 'So I thought I'd bring him down here to see what it was that *you* insisted on spending the hospital money on.'

Chris experienced a rush of surprise through his awkwardness. 'The playroom was your idea?'

Faith's head lifted proudly, making Chris want to applaud. 'It certainly was. A small amount of money was allocated from every department in the hospital and it has saved a fortune in bank nursing fees because the staff can bring their kids in here instead of staying off due to lack of childcare. And they are so much happier with the new arrangements that morale has shot up.'

There was a flash of pink on the other side of the glass wall. 'Faith!' shouted Molly.

Faith's eyes met Chris's. 'Do you mind if I say hello? It won't be long – I'm due in theatre.'

She was asking him. 'Of course not.' He shook Veronica's arm off.

The woman gave a sharp laugh. 'Exactly what I warned against. Staff are wasting time with their children instead of working. And this isn't even Dr Taylor's child.'

'I know,' said Chris. He was becoming very tired of this woman. 'She's mine. For the record, this excellently-provisioned playroom is one of the reasons I was so keen to take the post at Dale Head.'

Veronica's mouth opened and shut. She would now execute a complete *volte face*, thought Chris cynically. He was more interested in watching Faith crouch down next to Molly to look at a ladybird jigsaw puzzle.

'I need to get back to work, sweetheart,' she was saying, 'or I'll have patients lined up along the corridor on their operating trolleys. Have fun.'

Molly made a face, but the outburst Chris expected didn't come.

'Naturally,' said Veronica, 'once the nursery had been agreed I stipulated that it must be as well stocked as we could manage.' She slipped her arm through Chris's again. 'As it happens I do have one or two ideas on how to stretch your Obs & Gynie budget. Perhaps we could talk about it over lunch?'

In the playroom, Molly was waving Panda's arm to say goodbye to Faith. Her attention wandered and she saw Chris. 'Daddy!' she yelled happily. Then her face changed to fury as she took in Veronica's arm. She rushed towards the door, getting tangled in Faith's legs. 'Daddy! Want my daddy!'

Faith scooped the little girl up. Her eyes connected urgently with Chris. He nodded tersely through the glass, disengaging himself from Veronica without even thinking about it.

'And look,' said Faith, bringing Molly outside, 'here's Daddy coming to make sure you are having fun too.'

'Hello,' said Veronica. 'Aren't you a pretty little girl?'

Molly screamed louder. She knew a patronising tone of voice when she heard one.

'What a noise,' said Faith placidly. 'One quick kiss for Daddy then you pop back inside while he comes and sits in on an appointment with me. He won't be long.'

Molly glared balefully at Veronica. 'Will he be in your office?'

'Yes,' said Faith. 'The same office you've seen.'

'Just you and him?'

'Just me, him, my patient and a queue a mile long down the corridor.'

Molly gave a watery giggle and let Faith carry her back inside.

Chris turned to Veronica. 'I'm sorry. Perhaps we can reschedule.' He hurried off down the corridor with Faith, knowing his daughter was watching. 'Thank you,' he said, really grateful.

'I did it for Molly,' replied Faith in a clipped voice. 'Far be it for me to interfere, Chris, but standing outside the playroom with your arm round a woman Molly doesn't know was a pretty stupid thing to do.'

'You don't think that was *my* idea, do you?'

She slanted a look at him. 'You weren't trying any too hard to shake her off.'

It was true. He'd been loath to make an enemy of a person who could get his department extra budget. 'Money,' he said.

'Chris, this is a small hospital. People will talk.'

He sighed. 'You're right.' And Molly's reaction had reminded him all over again that he mustn't form any relationships until she was a lot more stable.

'Mind you, the way she was looking at you, Veronica would have given you the money for half a dozen new staff.'

'Faith! You can't object to me making friends with people who will be friends to the Department. Anyone would think you were jealous.'

'Jealous! Me?'

'Just joking,' he said.

106

'It might be funny to you but I...' Her pager sounded softly in her pocket. 'Help, I'm late.'

She lifted it to her ear, listened a moment and then looked at Chris. His senses came alert. The time for joking was over.

Her pace picked up to a jog. 'I don't believe it! Today of all days! Jared Carpenter, my junior registrar was about to perform a hysterectomy. Technically I'm observing. I'm to be his second. The patient is anaesthetised, Jared is all scrubbed up – and he's tripped over, fallen on his hand and dislocated two of his fingers! No way dare he operate now and the op needs to be done asap. Patient is asthmatic. We've been monitoring the case with the anaesthetist. I've really got to hurry.'

Chris found himself running alongside her. 'Are you going to let me help again?'

She looked at him in some irritation. 'Of course I am. A patient's care is at stake. I'd accept help from Attila the Hun if he was a qualified surgeon.'

'I'm a better surgeon than Attila the Hun. Let's go and see what we can do.'

Chapter Five

Faith suspected that neither she nor Chris had ever scrubbed up so quickly in their lives before. The patient was asthmatic, which always made anaesthesia a problem. This had to be done quickly. There was just time for them both to recheck the notes and the x-rays, and to confer with the anaesthetist. 'I don't want you to hurry,' the anaesthetist said, 'just be quick.'

'That's an anaesthetist's joke,' she told Chris. Then they entered the theatre.

The patient, Jenny Sullivan, was forty-five years old, had been suffering from fibroids with considerable distension and pain. After talking to her, and her GP it had been decided not only to remove her uterus but also her ovaries – as well as a hysterectomy she was to have an oophorectomy. She already had three children, was past child-bearing age and there was a history of ovarian cancer in her family. Best to remove the ovaries.

'I've watched you operate,' Chris said, 'and

I have every confidence in you, I thought you were brilliant. But you've never watched me work in the theatre except for that bit of closing. Would you like me to lead?' He saw her hesitate and added, 'This is entirely your decision and I will be happy with it.'

If she had been in doubt, then that remark would have convinced her. She nodded crisply. 'Very well. You lead.'

The patient was wheeled in. Faith saw Chris studying the x-rays illuminated on the wall behind them. 'Jared and I had decided on a vertical incision,' she said, 'the uterus is too bulky for comfort and the fibroids are massive.' This would mean that Jenny would have a more obvious scar – but safety was more important than beauty.

Chris grinned underneath his mask. 'I can do a bikini line incision,' he said, not boasting, but with quiet confidence. 'With the right help.'

'You've got it,' replied Faith.

They both looked down at the patient, swathed in green cloths, with only the necessary area of body exposed. Chris took up his scalpel, paused for that moment that Faith recognised so well. You were about to cut into a living body. No matter that you were trying to heal, it was an intrusion. Then

Chris made the first incision and such thoughts were banished.

Faith fitted the self-retaining retractors to hold the wound open. Chris then clamped, sealed and cut the ligaments that held the uterus in place. Then he dissected out the organ, prepared to remove it. Faith watched, assisted. Chris was good! His fingers moved quickly but surely. What he was doing would seem obvious and easy to an unknowing spectator. But Faith recognised the vast skill that was involved. She also noticed how well they worked together. She anticipated his wishes, knew what he was going to do next. The adrenalin sung in her veins as they worked. They were a good team.

And finally the excision was complete. The job had been done – well done. 'Do you want to close?' Chris asked her.

She shook her head. 'No. I like watching you work.'

So Chris closed, nodded to the anaesthetist. 'The job is all yours now.'

'Good to work with you both,' said the anaesthetist. 'You were quick.'

Faith and Chris drank coffee together afterwards. Jared had watched through the observation window and was full of praise.

He wasn't in any pain, he said, he'd had his hand x-rayed, there were no bones broken. He felt such a fool for tripping over, but said it had almost been worth it to watch them work.

'Who put your fingers back?' Faith asked him.

'Did it myself straight away. I just got hold of them and pulled.' He drained his own coffee. 'I'll be off to check on Mrs Sullivan's post-operative care. See you.'

And so Faith was left alone with Chris. Between them there was that bond that comes when two people know they have co-operated and done a good job in a tricky situation. It gave her the confidence to say, 'I hope you won't take offence, but you look exhausted. More than the op warranted. Trouble with Molly again?'

He sipped his coffee. 'You could say that. After she came home from seeing you last night she was almost the perfect child. Enjoyed her bath and she was soon asleep. But she woke up at four this morning and there was no calming her. No special reason, nothing had upset her – in fact just the opposite. She'd had a happy time with you. But old demons came back and neither of us got much sleep for the next couple of hours.' He shrugged. 'I just have to hope that it will pass. In time.'

'I'm sure it will. You'd better go, Chris. You said you wouldn't be long.' She hesitated. 'I'm really not interfering, but have you thought of buying her a pad and a set of crayons and encouraging her to use them? Sometimes it helps for children to express their feelings by drawing.'

'It's worth a try. She enjoyed drawing with you. Even if it does mean she'll want to draw instead of going to bed. And I hope you won't mind, but I wondered why you had crayons to hand?'

She hadn't expected this question, wasn't sure what to answer. After a short hesitation, she said, 'I used to draw and paint a lot. But I've not done any for the past few years.'

Uneasily, she saw that his eyes were now alert. He had realised there must have been some traumatic reason to make her give up. 'Any special reason why?' he asked.

'I had plenty to do here at hospital,' she said. 'Painting took a back seat and then just quietly faded away.' She could tell by his expression that he had not accepted her story but he was too courteous to say so. Time for her to distract him before he wanted to know more. 'Shoo,' she said briskly. 'Go and get Molly.'

Much to her relief, Chris wasn't in the next day. Just the weekend to go, then he would be her boss full time. It was going to be difficult.

It was. Chris instituted morning briefings that she thought wasted valuable time, then infuriatingly he drew up a rota showing when he was in charge and when Faith would take over that left her with *more* time than she was used to. He was scrupulous about dividing observations and admin with her and even magicked up a second junior registrar on a short-term transfer. Faith felt comprehensively out manoeuvred.

Jared had spread the word about Chris's theatre skills, so within the department he was treated with as much respect as in the wider hospital. Which was fine, thought Faith fairly, but the way her colleagues were falling over themselves to be nice to him, she didn't think she'd be missed when she left Dale Head to pursue her own career. And that was a tiny bit hurtful.

More of a problem would be Molly. She had taken to coming over in the early evenings, just for an hour or so to play and draw and give Chris a bit of a respite. After the fury she had shown on seeing her father apparently paying attention to Veronica – and Faith's tart comment on it, which she had regretted the moment it was out of her mouth – they had come to an unspoken agreement, working as colleagues, but preserving a distance between them when it came to their private lives. It was as if the fence between their gardens was a mental as well as physical barrier. Faith knew Chris couldn't risk getting involved in another deep relationship and Heaven knew it was the last thing on *her* mind. But she was coming to love his little girl and would miss her bright chatter. And when she was being honest with herself Faith was aware that the moments she and Chris spent during 'hand-over' time were assuming more importance than they should. She was worried about his well-being as well as Molly's.

She was in the canteen towards the end of the week – another side-effect of Chris's rota was that there was time for proper lunch-breaks – when Abbey Kirk plumped herself down next to her.

'Are you busy?' asked Abbey.

'Not for twenty minutes. What's up?'

'Your young neighbour, Molly Ford. At times she plays with the other kids, seems happy with them, is enjoying life like any five year old should. Then there are times like right now. She finds herself a corner, curls up in it and won't shift. She's been in the Wendy house for over an hour. I've tried half a dozen times to tempt her out – but she just won't have it. I ask you, a five-year-old Greta Garbo, just wanting to be alone?'

This was troubling. 'What does Chris say?'

'That she's had problems and to let her be.' Abbey sighed. 'If I try to force her out there's a scene and that upsets the others. So I just keep an eye on her and hope that she'll come back to normal. But she was murmuring your name when I went past just now, so I wondered…'

Faith found she was already on her feet. 'Of course. Poor little scrap.'

'You wouldn't say that if you'd heard her this morning. She's one confused kid. When she's good she's perfect. When she isn't–'

'I know. They live at the bottom of my garden, remember?'

'Must make it tricky. Jack took to Chris at once – said he was a gentleman. But it must be odd living next door to the man you're working with.'

'We keep home life and working life separate.'

Abbey looked at her shrewdly. 'You've got a lot in common. Roughly the same age, both single and...'

'Abbey! You're sounding like my sisters. We're colleagues and neighbours. That's all.'

'But you have got a soft spot for Molly?'

'Of course I have. That's why I'm coming with you now.'

Faith crouched at the opening to the Wendy house. 'Hello, Molly, I've come to see you. Will you come out?'

Molly was sitting right at the back, looking out. There was silence for a moment, then she said, 'You can come in if you want.'

'I wouldn't fit. Wendy houses are for little girls. If I got in there I'd be like a snail with a shell on my back.'

Molly gave a tiny giggle. 'But I like it in here,' she said.

'If you come out you can cuddle next to me for a while.' Faith moved backwards and wriggled down into a large bean bag like the one she had seen in Chris's lounge. 'There's plenty of room here for two.'

Molly sighed, then slowly came out of the Wendy house and burrowed close beside Faith. Faith put an arm round her. 'It's nice here, isn't it?' she said. 'Don't you want to

116

play with the other children?' Molly didn't speak, just shook her head.

'Why not?'

'Want to be with Daddy. Or with you.'

Faith winced even as she felt her heart melt. It was good to be wanted and she liked Molly. But the child shouldn't be dependent on her. It wouldn't be fair.

'You'll be with Daddy as soon as he finishes work. Meanwhile Hannah over there is having a teddy's tea party. You could take Panda.'

Molly looked dolefully across. 'But if I do, I'll have to play Hannah's way, not mine.'

Faith felt a rush of relief. Molly was simply having trouble adjusting to not being the biggest fish in the pond any more. 'Well, that's not too bad. You play Hannah's tea party her way, then maybe she can play fairies with you your way. And after that, you might be able to make up a game together.'

Molly looked unconvinced. 'I like playing my way all the time.'

'Well, yes, we all do. But...' Faith tried to think of something that would help her fit in. 'It's how life works, sweetheart. For instance, I was looking after Daddy's department before he got here, so I did it my way. But now he is in charge, he's doing things his way.

Some of my ideas he didn't see the point of – like going out to visit nervous patients in their own home before an operation – but he's sticking with them because I told him they work. And some of his ideas, I didn't see the point of – like having a meeting every morning so the whole team knows what everyone else is doing – but I tried it for a few days and he's right, it does make a difference. People feel more involved.'

Molly's small body was tense with concentration. 'All right,' she said eventually. 'I'll play tea parties with Hannah.'

Faith kissed her forehead. 'Good girl. Give people a chance and they'll give you a chance.'

'And then will you come and have tea with us at our house? Daddy said that if I wanted to invite anyone for tea, then I could.'

This was getting too difficult! 'I think he meant another little girl or boy,' Faith explained.

'But I've had tea at your house. And Daddy likes you. He says he likes you a lot.'

Just being nice for his daughter, Faith thought. Nothing else but that. She couldn't explain to Molly that she was worried what might happen if she spent too much time with Chris. Despising herself, she said what every adult said to a child when she couldn't think of an answer. 'We'll just have to see.'

She didn't see Chris that afternoon. It wasn't that she thought she'd be accused of interfering, but all the same she took care to be on the wards when he was due to finish for the day and pick Molly up.

It was a gorgeous sunny evening, the roads were quiet and she opened her car window to let the scents of summer blow in as she drove home. Usually, the well-loved hills surrounding her calmed her – but not this time. Thoughts, feelings, clouded her mind. She knew she had a problem, but she wasn't sure exactly what it was. Oh, what nonsense. Who was she kidding? Chris was the problem. She wanted to know him better. But she didn't want to get too close.

And having admitted that, there wasn't the usual feeling of peace and tranquillity when she arrived at her cottage. She didn't feel like preparing herself a meal. Of all things she felt lonely. Lonely! This was her haven, the place where she always felt safe. When the phone rang she hurtled across the room to pick it up. It would be Chris. She'd explain about Molly and the Wendy house.

'Hi, Sis!' Hope's cheerful tones rang down

the line. 'Telephone consultation. I need the advice of the best Obs and Gynie person I know. Feel free to send in a bill.'

Faith beat back the flicker of disappointment. Hope was a midwife, attached to one of the GP practices that fed into Dale Head hospital. Usually she would refer medical problems to one of the GPs. But Faith knew all the GPs – and knew they would be only too pleased to have her expert advice. 'What's the problem?' she asked.

'I've got a primagravida out in a farm up Yallendale valley. There have been no problems so far, she's done everything right. But I have this *feeling*, you know how it is.'

Faith's brow wrinkled. She did know. Hope's "feelings" were often accurate. 'Got the case notes there?'

'Of course.'

'Read them out to me.' Carefully she made notes as Hope read. 'It doesn't sound as if there's anything to worry about. From those results I'd guarantee that your patient is going to be fine.'

'I know,' Hope said. 'But I get these hunches every now and again, so if you can hold on to the notes and let your subconscious work on them in the next few weeks I'd be grateful. Now, what's worrying you?'

'Worrying me? Nothing.'

'Nonsense. I know you. I can tell by your voice there's something wrong.'

'There isn't. I'm tired. I'm thinking through life changes and I haven't eaten yet. As soon as I feel like cooking, I'll–'

'One of Charity's patients left a whole salmon on our doorstep. There's loads left and it needs eating. I'll bring it round.'

'But I'm knackered! I just want peace.'

'So sit down and put your feet up. I'll be there in fifteen minutes.'

The phone went dead. Faith glared at it. She'd heard the concern in her sister's voice and of course it was good to be loved but...

Hope arrived: energetic, good-humoured and just slightly too busy. Faith's heart sank. Was her sister having trouble with her love life again? She got no chance to ask because Hope was chattering ten to the dozen about the GP practice, the course Charity was on this week and the neighbour who had asked her to feed their menagerie while they were away.

They sat on the patio to eat the salmon and a tossed salad. 'Do you remember how you used to make us use a whisk to mix the salad dressing?' Hope asked as she placed a small glass dish on the table.

'I still do. Home-made dressing always tastes better than shop bought.'

'Ha! It used to make my wrist hurt so now I compromise. This is home made dressing made with a battery driven whisk. Try it!'

Faith took a roll, dipped it into the dressing, tasted. 'That is good,' she acknowledged. The sisters smiled at each other.

Her phone rang again.

'Faith.' It was Chris and his tone was curt. 'Molly would like to come over, but I want to talk to you as well.'

Faith felt her stomach clench. 'I've got a visitor. Can it wait?'

She could have sworn she heard him growl, but she must have imagined it. 'Tomorrow?'

'Yes, okay, I ... ooops, too late.' A blue-clad figure was already rushing joyfully towards the fence.

Chris cursed. 'Sorry, she's slippery as an eel tonight. I'll come and get her.'

'No, don't. I can manage.' But he'd already rung off and Hope was setting off interestedly for the bottom of the garden.

Molly had stopped, just through the gap. 'Who are you?' she said, staring at this stranger, her lower lip wobbling.

Hope hunkered down. 'I'm Faith's sister.

Are you coming to play?'

Molly nodded, but looked anxiously up the garden towards Faith and then behind her towards where her father was catching her up.

Faith and Chris reached the fence at the same moment. For a moment the barrier might not have been there at all as they both held their breath to see how Molly would deal with Hope.

'More visitors. How lovely,' said Hope, straightening up. 'You must be Chris. Would you like some salmon? And a drink? I've been wanting to meet the man who got my sister's job.'

'Hope!' Faith gasped.

Chris shook his head, and Faith saw the amusement in his eyes. 'Now I know what I'm missing not having a family,' he said. 'Faith, I envy you.'

It was more than she did at the moment, especially when Molly fixed her eyes on Hope and said in a serious voice, 'She was only looking after the department for Daddy. Sometimes they work Faith's way and sometimes they work Daddy's way. Mostly Daddy's, but Faith doesn't mind now because it's better.'

Faith closed her eyes. 'Can we start this

evening again, please?'

'Don't be silly,' said Hope with a grin. 'Go and put the kettle on and make a cup of tea for your guests. I'll entertain them while you're gone.'

'I've got a better idea,' said Faith. 'You go and put the kettle on and I'll do the entertaining.'

'Thanks, but we're not stopping,' began Chris, but Molly was already speaking.

'Want orange, not tea.' She studied Hope a moment more then took her hand. 'I know where it is.'

'Golly,' said Faith, watching them trot up the path.

Chris seemed equally amazed. 'There's a family resemblance to you. Perhaps that's why.'

'Could be. I apologise for my sister's bluntness.'

'It was refreshing.' He cleared his throat. 'Abbey and Molly both told me you'd talked to her today. It seems I have to thank you again.'

'She's taking a while to adjust, that's all.'

He rubbed his chin. 'Did you really not agree with the briefings to begin with?'

Oh, *why* had she said that to Molly? 'I didn't see the point. But I do now. I'm cross because I didn't think of it myself.'

'Why would you? I got the idea from one of my previous Heads of Department. You've only really known Freddie Myers.'

Was that another dig at her inexperience outside Dale Head? Faith sighed. She was tired and conscious of not making a good showing.

Chris put his hand on her shoulder. 'Faith, don't hold it against me that I've worked in more places than you.'

His touch was warm and comforting. His voice was gentle. Faith blew her nose and shook herself free before she could admit to wanting more. 'Don't let Molly see you. Maybe you should stay that side of the fence to drink your tea.'

'No need,' he said, swinging himself across and glancing at her in a way that was too frank for comfort. 'These days I'm carrying the damn fence round with me.'

And just what did he mean by that? Faith pondered the question, noting with some misgiving the way all the way through the conversation that followed, her sister was taking in the fact that Molly knew her way around the house, had asked immediately for crayons and that Faith herself knew how Chris liked his tea.

'We work together, okay?' she hissed after an unsubtly warm commendation on her homemaking skills from Hope.

'Of course you do,' said her sister soothingly. 'Well, I must go. There's a medical journal calling my name at home.'

'Pity it didn't call earlier,' muttered Faith.

If Hope thought she was being tactful, she was thwarted by Chris also getting to his feet and saying they should be leaving. Never one to be outmanoeuvred, she continued, 'But first we need to tidy up. Come on, Molly. Let's put the crayons away.'

'Sorry,' said Faith awkwardly to Chris. 'This is what comes of Hope not having a love-life of her own to concentrate on at present.'

'No matter. She's not to know that we—'

A shout pierced the evening stillness.

'Daddy! Oh, Daddy! Come and see!'

Molly, when they raced to find her, was standing in the back scullery and was revolving, entranced at Faith's garden painting.

'Goodness, this is lovely,' said Chris. He looked around at the painted walls.

Faith's mood plummeted even further. 'It's just a mural,' she said. 'I had the idea a few years ago that I wanted to bring the garden into the house. So I started painting it and – and it grew.' And standing here with the cold growing inside her brought it all back. Mike, leaning against the doorjamb as she crouched trying to get a flower or a bug right, teasing her, loving her.

'What's a muriel?' asked Molly.

'A mural is a wall painting. Like this one.' Faith could sense Chris studying her, trying to divine why she was so still. She forced herself to smile.

'I want a muriel on my wall,' said Molly. 'You said I could have what I wanted in my bedroom, Daddy. I want a garden just like this.'

Faith barely heard her. The pain was still there. It would never leave. She had been so happy when she painted this, and then within a few weeks of finishing, Mike had been dead and the life had gone out of her. She turned to switch out the light. 'Let's go back into the–'

'There's a ladybird! And a daffodil. What's this flower, Faith?'

The little voice was insistent. Faith turned, her hand still outstretched towards the switch. 'That's a tulip, darling. Come and–'

'And these are roses, I know them. What are those tall ones? They're as tall as Daddy!'

Torture. This was torture. Faith didn't want to remember painting this. She focused. 'Those are hollyhocks. I'll show you them for real outside tomorrow.'

Molly let out a peal of laughter. 'Hollyhocks is a funny name. When I'm as tall as Daddy will I be a Mollyhock?'

There was a sharp ache in Faith's chest. She found she was smiling and trying not to cry at the same time.

'Faith?' said Chris in a concerned voice. 'Are you all right?'

She made herself answer. 'I'm fine. Cold. Been outside too long.'

A sharp glance said he didn't believe her, but, 'Then get into your warm kitchen. Right now. Time to go home, Molly. Say goodbye to Hope and Faith.' With fast, understated authority he got everyone moving. For a moment Faith was terrified he and Molly would be offered a lift – the little girl being enchanted by Hope's bright pink car – but Hope found herself being waved off alone.

'I want a pink car,' said Molly.

'Just as soon as you grow up and learn to drive,' Chris assured her. He put his hand on Faith's shoulder and said under his breath, 'Give me an hour to get bedtime over, then if you want to talk, ring me.'

Faith nodded, knowing she wouldn't. Alone again, the memory of his hand was the only warm thing about her. She knew she was being a coward. She gritted her teeth and went back into the scullery. Once more, all that past love flowed around her. What would Mike want for her now? She remembered his zest for life, the twinkle in his eyes, and thought perhaps she knew. But it was so hard admitting it. Her gaze fell on the charcoal drawings she'd done the other day. She hesitated, then took the pad into the lounge with her. Sketching wasn't painting. Sketching was cathartic. Sketching she could do.

Back in his house, preparing his chattering daughter for bed, Chris felt torn. Torn and very confused. Usually when Molly was good, he loved the time he spent with her. He should be enjoying it now – and he was. But in the back of his mind was the affectionate sparring between Faith and her sister before everything had suddenly gone wrong, and in the front of his mind – almost blotting everything else out – was that wrongness itself. Faith, unhappy. Faith, unhappy and cold and looking as if something unbelievably precious had been wrenched from her.

Chris told himself to calm down, to address the situation logically. First, the teasing between the sisters. That had unsettled him, making him think how pleasant it would be to be part of a family like that. He had been an only child, and now Molly was an only child. Neither of them would have that extra dimension, that playful love which could nevertheless hit home without offence.

And then there was Faith. At the sight of her sudden, bloodless face he'd wanted so badly to put his arms around her, to fold her against his chest just as he held Molly in the inarticulate aftermath of a tantrum.

He shook his head. It wasn't possible. Look how Molly had reacted at the sight of Veronica Beresford's arm tucked into his. He had to care for Faith from a distance, to forget the feel of her bare shoulder against his palm, forget Hope's suggestions of barbeques and picnics, and think of his daughter. He had to do what was best for her.

But Molly was fond of Faith. She was talking about her now as she got ready for bed and picked out a story book about a garden fairy for him to read. Maybe...

No! He had to stamp down hard on that possibility! There had been no sign of Lorraine's instability when he married her. It was the trauma of depression following Molly's birth that had triggered it. The same could happen with any other woman. He couldn't take the risk. He couldn't expose Molly to the possibility of another relationship crumbling around her just when she had begun to feel secure.

And then Chris gave a short, humourless laugh. All this angst on his part – but there was also Faith herself. What made him think there might ever be a relationship to go wrong? Faith was uncomfortable with the attraction between them. She was frightened of committing herself. It was obvious that something in her life had left an emotional scar. Probably something to do with that lovely garden painting around the walls of her utility room. He shouldn't open up the wound, even though he desperately wanted to know what the matter was.

He read the story to Molly with part of him still thinking about Faith. She made a small snuffly noise and he realised she had fallen asleep while he'd been sitting here holding her hand. As he always did when he left her at night, he bent over to kiss her forehead. Molly was and must be central to his life. There was only one conclusion. It hurt, but he had to keep a friendly distance from Faith.

He walked downstairs, poured the small whisky he sometimes allowed himself at the end of the day, went to sit in the darkened conservatory. He could see the lights in Faith's cottage. His hand hovered over his mobile. If she'd regained her customary calm, she wouldn't want to be dragged out of it. But if she was sitting there, cold and alone...

He had to know. He phoned, heard her voice. 'Are you all right?' he asked.

She didn't answer straight away. He heard a sigh. 'I'm fine. I'll see you tomorrow.' A pause. 'Thank you, Chris.'

She rung off. Chris looked out over the dark garden. There was a fence between their two cottages – a symbol of what was keeping them apart. Molly might pay no attention to the fence, but Chris needed to remember it was there.

Chapter Six

Chris had always started work early. If he could get to his desk just half an hour before the rest of the staff began to arrive, then he was ahead on points. He was enjoying working in this new hospital. There was a vast amount to do of course, he was wearied every night. But the work was good, he could count on his department not to throw major problems at him without warning, and he was generous enough to know that this was mostly down to the efficient teamwork that Faith had put in place over the past few years.

Faith. Chris's stomach clenched. Faith was the one troubling item in his day-to-day life. Every glimpse and every thought of her made him want to know her better. It was like an itch he didn't dare scratch. There was Molly to think of. And the memory of life with Lorraine. Never would he risk going through anything like that again, not with any woman. But how did he balance the need to keep Faith at a distance with his concern about what was going on beneath her surface control?

Today, as ever, there was a pile of mail on his desk. Some was for him, some still addressed to his predecessor. Most of it went instantly into the waste-paper basket. Did any doctor respond to the barrage of advertising material that arrived on his desk? He opened another envelope, brightening when he saw the logo for Hadrian's Wall hospital. At least this one would have some medical interest. But as he read it he felt the pit of his stomach drop away.

In standard hospitalese it stated that Dr Faith Taylor had applied for the position of Head of the Obstetrics and Gynaecology Department. The board would be obliged if a reference could be supplied.

Chris was thunderstruck. Also very angry. All right, so Faith was upset about losing out to him as head of *this* department, but she wasn't even giving him a chance! He tightened his hands on the request, getting more furious by the minute. Had she no idea of etiquette? Applying for a new job without even doing him the courtesy of informing him? He'd thought they were getting along better than that! Without giving himself time to think, he stormed down the corridor to her office.

Her smile as he strode in swiftly turned to concern. 'What is it?'

'This.' He slammed down the letter on her desk.

'Oh.' She looked embarrassed.

Was that the best she could do? Just 'Oh'. He balled his fists. 'Exactly so. And you were going to tell me when? Faith, if you've got problems with the way I'm running this department, just say so! This is a delightful way of finding out my Senior Registrar is unhappy with me, I must say.'

Her eyes widened. Then she folded her arms and leaned back in her chair. Her voice became clipped and professional. 'One, Freddie told me about the opening and I applied before you even arrived here. Two, I put Freddie himself down as a referee, not you, as you can see if you look at that letter properly. Three, I am entitled to a career of my own. And four, if I was unhappy with my working conditions, believe me, I would tell you.'

Chris stood there, unable to move. One part of him was furiously refuting everything she had just said. The other – taking in the admin details at the top of the letter – was realising, belatedly and horribly, that she was right. He was appalled at himself. What had he just done? He'd reacted with his emotions, not with his head.

'Hell,' he said inadequately.

As they stared at each other, two things struck him. Firstly, Faith deserved to get the post. She would be terrific at it: the hospital and the patients would benefit. Secondly, he didn't want her to go. She was an extremely good doctor. She was being an enormous help to him as he took over the reins of this new department. Without her he could still do the work – but it would be so much harder.

Then, as her eyes softened, he realised that he'd missed the most important thing of all. The thing his heart had instantly known. The reason he'd been so thrown, so unreasonably hurt. He wanted her close by. Not for any professional reason, not because she was a friend to Molly, but because when she was near, he was aware that one day there would be more to life. And that was unforgivable, because there wasn't any way he could make any sort of promise to her.

'I'm sorry,' he said, summoning up some vestige of normality. His voice was more of a croak than his usual tone, but it was a start. 'I was out of order. Jumping to conclusions.'

'Apology accepted.' And now she stood, putting her hand on his upper arm. 'Chris, I don't mean to interfere but do you think perhaps you are working too hard? You were here when I came in and you haven't had a proper lunch break for days. You've taken over stuff that I ought to do as well as your own work.'

How unfair was that! He'd busted a gut over the schedule to make it fairer on her! *'You* were doing it all,' he pointed out, trying not to sound aggrieved.

'Yes, which is how I know it's too much! With me a lot of it could be dealt with routinely because I've been here so long, but you have to feel your way round hospital politics as well as learning about every new patient. And you have Molly to take care of as well. Chris, you'll make yourself ill.'

'I'm a bit like you. I find peace, calm, satisfaction in work.'

'In work done well, yes. But nobody can do their best when they're shattered.' She gave a tentative grin. 'This is your senior registrar talking. You should listen to me, you know.'

Her hand was still on his arm. He could feel her genuine concern for him. Hardly knowing what he did, he covered her fingers with his own. 'You are one generous woman. In a moment I will make us both a coffee and then perhaps you could come along to my office, we will start today over and discuss dividing up the work to give us *both* a sensible schedule. How's that?'

'That sounds good.' She cleared her throat. 'And I apologise for not mentioning the Hadrian's Wall job. To tell you the truth, I couldn't find the right moment.'

'Faith–' No, he couldn't say anything more. Even if he had just realised that life without her would be interminably grey. Molly, Lorraine, all his previous failings … battered at his mind. 'Nothing,' he said. 'I'll get that coffee. Five minutes, okay?'

What had *that* all been about? Faith looked at the closed door, her legs shaky and her feelings in turmoil. She hoped she'd hidden her flash of insight well, but Chris's fury had not seemed to her like impersonal interest. The back of her hand could still feel the slight roughness of his palm, the warmth. There had been that stricken, horrified look in his eyes when he realised he'd jumped to false conclusions. It had called out to her, begged her to ease his embarrassment.

She drew a deep breath. She would go into

his room now and be absolutely professional. Pretend they really were starting this morning over. But she didn't think she'd be able to forget that moment when she'd locked eyes with Chris and known passion was simmering just beneath the surface. Her whole body had suddenly turned molten. She'd *wanted* to go further and had seen an answering flash in him. She didn't think he would be able to forget either. What on earth were they going to do?

For now at least, they ignored it. In his office, after going through the rota, Chris mentioned casually that he had received a letter from Hadrian's Wall hospital asking for a reference. 'Of course I'll supply one but I'll also write to Freddie for his comments. He's known you far longer than I have, his opinion will carry more weight. And I know he thinks highly of you.' He paused a moment and then added, 'On a professional level, I'd be sorry to see you go. If you are successful, would you still live in Fell View cottage?'

She shook her head. 'Not possible. It's a reasonable journey in good conditions, but the weather can blow up very quickly in the Lake District. I'd need to be near my work in case of emergencies.'

He gave a tiny intake of breath. 'You'd miss your sisters and your friends.'

She shook her head again. 'Not with phones and email and cars each.'

'Molly would miss you.' Tiny pause. 'And so would I.'

Professionally? Or personally? She held his eyes, moistened her lips. 'She'll settle, Chris. You'll make friends here. And the post isn't vacant until the New Year anyway.'

He looked down. His hand moved almost reluctantly to another letter on his desk. 'There's also this. It's a day conference at Hadrian's Wall hospital towards the end of the week to discuss government proposals aimed at making the regional Obs & Gynie provision work more efficiently: how we can share work, liaise with GPs and local health centres, that sort of thing. How we would manage if an emergency situation arose in the region. Freddie booked me in for it before he left, but it seems to me that as you know far more about the health provision around here than I do, it would be sensible for you to attend as Dale Head's representative and report back to the rest of us.' He smiled bleakly. 'And if you are as efficient as I suspect you will be, it won't do your selection chances with the Hadrian's Wall board any harm either.'

'Thank you,' she said quietly. She smiled bleakly. It was another way in which he was a better head of department then Freddie. Her old boss would have gone for the importance of representing the hospital; Chris wanted what was best for it.

'There's one last thing,' said Chris. 'I wouldn't ask, except...'

Faith was pulled out of her introspection at his tone. He seemed at once anxious, uneasy and almost ashamed. 'What is it?'

'Molly. I'm sorry, Faith, but she's talking as if the garden mural in her bedroom is an established fact. Could you ... would it be possible at all for you to paint her one?'

Paint another garden? Faith's hand moved in instinctive denial.

Chris was continuing. 'I have, of course, no idea how long it would take. And it was obvious that something in your garden room had upset you badly, so I'll understand if you say no. There must be a decorator somewhere who can do it for her.'

He was expecting her to refuse. And he was being very tactful about not prying. 'I ... it's difficult, Chris,' she said, distressed.

'I gathered it might be. But from my point of view as a loving father, I had to ask. It was also to warn you to be prepared when Molly tells you about it as if it's a settled fact.'

Faith bowed her head. *Would it be so very dreadful?* To paint a garden for a little girl who desperately needed to be happy and settled in her new home? 'Let me think about it, Chris.'

'Of course.'

It took Faith just over an hour to drive the fifty miles to Hadrian's Wall hospital for the conference. That would be easily manageable for sister-visits if she did get the Consultant job. The thought gave her a slightly apprehensive feeling in her chest, but she gave herself a pep talk on how she must make this opportunity work for her. The countryside was beautiful, the hospital had an excellent clinical reputation, she would be happy in her work. And it would be her own department.

But no longer would Chris and Molly be living at the bottom of her garden.

It was a good session during the morning. Faith contributed well and had the satisfaction of knowing people were listening to the points she made. One of the speeches was given by Tommy Case, Freddie's friend, the soon-to-retire Obs & Gynie consultant and head of department here. She had met him before and liked him. During the lunch break, Tommy steered her towards the comfortable seating.

'I've worked for years to establish this department,' he told her, 'and I'm proud of what I have done. I want someone here who I can trust to carry on with my work. Freddie has told me a lot about you, Faith. From what he says, you are the sort of person I'd like to see at Hadrian's Wall.'

'That's – that's very kind. Thank you.' Faith was shocked to be singled out like this. Her eyes slid to the others in the room, noticing them casting curious glances her way.

'Just you remember it. I know it's the hospital board that does the appointing, but I'm well in with them, they listen to my opinion – and I'm a lot less likely to leave things to chance as Freddie was.'

Faith didn't know what to say. 'Thank you again.'

He studied her for a moment. 'I've been listening to you today. You care about the area, but more importantly, you care about the people who would actually be doing all the work we're cavalierly dreaming up for them to do. Don't lose that quality. It's what stops a doctor being just a mask.'

Faith prepared for the afternoon session in a sober frame of mind. Yes, she cared about people. Even here, she'd had an email exchange with Jared about three of the patients in the ward at home. Would that level of involvement be lessened with the step up to head of department? She tried recalling Chris's spreadsheet of allocated time. Instead all she could think of was his arm brushing hers as they both bent to look at it on his desk. No! She didn't want this! She didn't want to lay herself open for pain again. But part of her couldn't help hoping Molly wouldn't be too disappointed not to play with her this evening.

Chris looked at his stormy daughter in desperation. 'Sweetheart, I can't help it that Faith is away today. Do you want to draw with me instead?'

Molly scowled. 'All right.' She got out a big sheet of paper and began crayoning thick black wax all over it.

He watched her worriedly. 'Are you making a picture?'

For answer, she crayoned harder.

'What does Faith do when you draw?' he asked in a carefully offhand voice.

'She draws too. Or she uses her computer.

Or reads a book.' The black was covering quite a lot of the sheet by now.

'Do you mind if I phone work, then?'

'That's okay.'

He rang Jared Carpenter quickly, only to find that Faith had already been in touch regarding her patients. Jared said she'd told him the meetings had gone very well and she would put together a summary for Dale Head staff tomorrow. Nice of her to phone *me*, thought Chris grumpily.

Molly had finished her picture and was looking at it with satisfaction. It was mostly black with a small, uncrayoned bit in the centre in which she had drawn a girl blob, a pink panda blob and a lot of multicoloured dots.

Chris stared at it in total perplexity, wondering if he should be ringing the child psychologist urgently. 'That's nice. What are the dots?'

To his astonishment, Molly giggled, her good humour restored. 'Fairies, of course. Like in my story. They're in my cave with me and Panda.' She squirmed down from the table and fetched one of her current favourite books, *The Forest Fairies Anthology*.

Chris pulled her onto his lap. 'Silly me. Of course they are. Who shall we read about today? Maple, Pine, Fern or Bracken?'

Silently, he blessed Faith. Suggesting Molly draw whenever she was unhappy was really working. Lorraine had never thought of anything like that. But if he'd tried harder to understand Lorraine, supported her a bit more, made more allowances for her illness... Why was it so hard for him to draw a line under this? Why couldn't he just accept that what was done was done? Why couldn't he move on the way she had?

It was a couple of days later that Faith and Chris had their first serious falling out over a patient. She knew that medicine was an art as much as it was a science, that one doctor's prescribed treatment might differ considerably from another's and both could be right. But this time she was sure Chris was wrong because it wasn't really a medical thing – it was a social problem.

Pregnant women came into the hospital for regular check-ups. They would usually be seen by a midwife, but if there were any problems they'd be referred to a doctor. En route to the Delivery Suite, Faith recognised one of the clinic patients as a woman she had seen herself the previous month. Rosie Beckett, standing gossiping outside the doorway.

Rosie always had time for a gossip. In fact she had time for little else. And she had put on weight. Not a good thing.

'Ooh, Doctor Taylor, nice to see you. I've just had that new doctor, Doctor Ford. Isn't he lovely?'

'Mr Ford is a very good doctor,' Faith said, remembering Chris had insisted on taking his turn as duty doctor. 'How are you keeping, Rosie?'

'I'm doing all right. He's dead good looking, isn't he?'

'Keeping up with your medication?'

Rosie shifted. 'Well, yes. Sort of.'

Faith sighed. Rosie was diabetic, which was not a good condition when you were pregnant. But with a properly controlled diet, just sufficient of the right sort of exercise, careful self-monitoring and above all absolute precision in taking her medication – Rosie should be all right. Otherwise, the life of both mother and baby could be threatened. 'Sort of?' she asked.

'Dr Ford said I had to take more care now I'm in my second tri ... trimester. Look at this prescription. And what I've got to do.'

Faith looked and blanched. Everything there she agreed with. Self-monitoring, measure blood glucose several times daily, keep it tightly controlled. Short-acting insulin before meals, long-acting insulin at night. Now four times a day instead of two. And the diet! 'Are you going to manage all this, Rosie? Should I arrange for the District Nurse to make regular visits?'

Rosie looked sullen. 'Her? Stuck-up cow. I remember her from school, she was a pain then. She's been to see me and I told her not to come again.'

'But you have the baby to think of. You really do need her help.'

'I can manage.'

Faith knew something of the family. Rosie was married to an oilrig worker, there was no shortage of money but he was away much of the time. Like now. She lived in the same street as her father, who kept a vague eye on her – mostly whenever he wanted a free meal. Her mother was dead. Not an ideal home situation for a scatterbrain like Rosie.

'Will you be very careful to follow these instructions exactly?'

Rosie looked resentful. 'Don't you start. Everyone's getting on at me.'

'Because everyone's worried about you.'

'Like I said, I can manage.' Rosie didn't like it when people told her what to do. She walked away.

Faith wondered for a moment, then walked into the Delivery Suite and phoned Chris. 'Chris, you've just seen Rosie Becket. She's just started on her second trimester and she's a diabetic.'

'That's right, not easy to forget. A woman who likes to talk. Why are you interested?'

Faith took a deep breath. 'I think you've made a mistake. She showed me the prescription and the instructions you gave her. I know Rosie and there is no way she'll manage to follow them. And she's fallen out with the District Nurse.'

She could tell that Chris didn't like being told that he had made a mistake. Well, who did? Perhaps it hadn't been very tactful to start by saying that he had made a mistake. But she knew she was right.

'Faith, I did go to a lot of trouble to explain the dangers of not following the instructions to her. And I'm sure I got the message across.'

'You got it across for now. She'll remember every word you said. Till tomorrow that is. Then she won't be so sure.'

Chris sighed. 'We just have to do the best we can with our patients,' he said. 'Sometimes they are their own worst enemy. What would you have me do? Admit her to a ward? We need all the beds we have got.'

'She wouldn't stay anyway.'

'Precisely. Faith, there is nothing we can do.'

'You're the consultant. Your decision.' She rang off.

Now she was angry. Why wouldn't he take her advice? These were people she knew and she knew she was right.

She spoke to him with freezing courtesy for the rest of the day and was irritated when he refused to be upset, treating her in his usual friendly fashion. For an awful moment she wondered if she might be wrong. But she knew she wasn't.

Next day she waited behind after the morning briefing, determined to ask him very politely to think again about Rosie Beckett. But she didn't need to. He smiled as he took in her expression. 'Faith, I do love how concerned you are over every single patient. You've got that look on your face that says that you know you are right and you're going to explain why – whether I want to hear it or not. You're going to tell me that you're worried about Rosie Beckett. And I agree that you could be right to be worried.'

Faith was a bit thrown by this, especially

as he was smiling as he spoke. She had been expecting a fight. 'Er, yes,' she said.

'I did pay attention to what you said. I called to see Rosie last night on my way home. You were right, she was already muddled with the instructions.'

'You called to see her?' Faith was surprised. Not many consultants would do this unless it was absolutely necessary.

He looked at her wryly. 'You were the one who told me seeing patients in their own home often tells you far more than seeing them in a consulting room.'

Now she felt uncomfortable, she had misjudged him. He had listened. He did care for his patients as much as she did. 'So what do you think is best to do now?' she asked.

He was looking genuinely pleased with himself for having solved a problem her way, rather than relying on a faceless team of professionals. 'I remembered what you said about this being a tight community and that people looked out for each other. When I collected Molly, I had a talk with Abbey. She knows even more about the people around here than you do, and that's saying something. Anyway, she told me Rosie's mother-in-law lives in the same village but she hasn't seen much of Rosie herself because she disapproves of Rosie's father who is often over there. She thinks he's a drunken ne'er-do well.'

'She could be right.'

'But when I told her that her first grandchild's life could be at risk, she got angry with herself. She decided she had to take a more active part in her family's life. From now on she'll be round at Rosie's house twice a day to make sure Rosie is taking all her medication and following all my instructions. I gave her a copy of them.'

'Do you think it will work?'

'Yes, I do.' He smiled again. 'If it comes to a contest of wills, I would back Mrs Beckett senior against Mrs Beckett junior and her drunken father any day.'

Now Faith felt even more off-balance. She was cross with herself for misjudging Chris, pleased for Rosie, and shamefully bothered that Chris had proved he could sort out Dale Head community problems without her help. 'Congratulations,' she said, trying not to sound grudging. 'That was truly brilliant on your part.'

He grinned. 'Not me. You pointed out what was likely to happen. I didn't give it a thought before that. You were right and I was wrong.'

Faith gave a weak smile. 'You're being generous.'

'Not at all. I'm just beginning to recognise that it's true that this hospital is almost like a family.' His voice lowered, she realised that he had abandoned his semi-serious, joking tone. He took her hand, shocking and confusing her. 'We're a great team, Faith. We work so well together. Don't fight me.'

'I'm not.' And she wasn't. She'd come here all fired up and he'd disarmed her. He was a good community doctor as well as a good surgeon. A few more weeks and he wouldn't need her at all. That was great. It meant if she got the Hadrian's Wall job, Dale Head wouldn't suffer. So why did she feel so flat? Why did him holding her hand make her want to cry?

'Faith?' He had a half-smile on his face. Almost tender.

She pulled her hand away, rubbed it distractedly. 'I don't know what to say, Chris. You're doing great.' Another quick breath. 'I have a clinic in ten minutes. See you later.'

She was running away and she knew it. Something was going to come to a head between them soon and for the first time in her life she didn't know how she was going to react. It wasn't just unsettling – it was downright terrifying. For some reason, one of her parents' favourite songs, an old pop song, popped into her head. *Que sera sera*. In other words: whatever will be will be. And there was another line in it indicating that the future wasn't theirs to see. Her haphazard parents had always drawn comfort from the idea. Faith shook her head. There might be truth there but she would much prefer to see where she was going, thank you very much.

Chris knelt by the bath, poured water over his daughter's head and shoulders. Molly shrieked with pleasure. She loved water. It struck him that they had not been swimming since they had moved, the past few weeks had been too busy to find where the nearest baths were. Or, as it was summer, why not bathe in a lake or river somewhere? He must ask Faith where would be a good place.

Faith. He relied upon her so much. Professionally certainly, no consultant could wish for a better senior registrar. But Faith had also helped him settle in the community, had introduced him to people he could rely on, had explained how life was different here from the always hurrying, buzzing city.

'When is Faith going to paint my garden?' asked Molly, uncannily picking up her father's thoughts.

He didn't know that she was. 'We haven't asked her yet. Did you see her today?'

'Yes. She said she would be working very late so I couldn't go over there after tea, but I could go there tomorrow. I was playing with Hannah and Luke and John and we all did ring-a-ring of roses and all fell down together.'

So that was why she hadn't made a fuss this afternoon, thought Chris ruefully. It had been Faith's influence all the time. She was good for both of them. He remembered this morning when he'd been so full of pleasure that he was learning a new way of working with patients on the ground, so to speak, that he couldn't help being less guarded with her than normal. He remembered the way her hand had trembled in his.

But there was Molly. And the ever-present spectre of Lorraine.

He took a resolute breath as he lifted Molly out of the bath and started to towel her dry. He'd ask about the mural tomorrow. Invite Faith to tea and to look at Molly's room. They were both sensible. They could do this.

Chapter Seven

The message was on her desk when she arrived. In Chris's firm, energetic writing, it asked whether she had thought any more about the mural.

That was thoughtful of him. He wasn't influencing her by asking face to face. He was giving her plenty of leeway to come up with a reason why she shouldn't paint it. But she had to stop running away some time. She picked up the phone. Two minutes later she was armed with an invitation to tea and the sensation that she might just have stepped into the deep end without warning.

She was visiting Chris as a friend, so she wanted to look nice. But casual. And it was warm, so a white t-shirt and light blue chinos. There had been an odd text from Chris on her phone during the afternoon. *When you come over – go to hole in fence.* So she did. And to her surprise there was a new little gate. No longer would Molly – or anyone – have to wriggle through the gap and risk tearing clothes. She looked at it, unsure how she felt.

Still, she went through and walked up to Chris's house. 'Where did that gate come from?' she asked.

'I phoned Jack Kirk as soon as you said yes and asked him if he could fix one up. If it doesn't work, he can reinstate the fence. I thought it might be more convenient. A gate is far easier for carrying stuff from cottage to cottage. But as I say, if you don't like it...'

'I like it,' she said.

She had brought a few things with her: tape measure, a sketching pad, pencils, and a knife for scratching away at the surface of the wall to find what was underneath. Her mural had to have a firm base.

Molly was ecstatic. 'I'm going to have a garden! With flowers and ladybirds and a big tree and butterflies and fairies.'

'Fairies?' Faith had an ominous feeling about this.

'Fairies. Like in my stories. Daddy reads them to me.'

'Tea is ready,' said Chris diplomatically.

They had eaten and were playing a board game with Molly when the phone rang. Molly looked at it crossly. Phones meant attention was being taken away from her.

'Chris Ford,' said Chris, answering it. 'Hi Jared, what's that? An accident? Where?'

As he listened, scribbling notes, Faith saw his face change. It was obvious what was about to happen. She looked back at Molly, fiercely throwing the dice. She had a minute to make her decision.

'Emergency,' said Chris, looking harassed. 'I've got to go in. A woman in her third trimester has been involved in a car crash. Extensive injuries to the abdomen as well as the rest of the body. There's a general surgeon starting work on her at once. Jared says the foetus is still viable but there are signs of distress. He thinks that there might need to be an early Caesarian. C'mon, Molly, let's grab your emergency bag. Have I ever told you how much I bless that playroom, Faith?'

'Would you like me to stay?' asked Faith.

Chris stopped in the act of putting his shoes on.

'I mean it,' she said. 'Molly and I can finish the game, then I'll put her to bed. She can tell me where everything is. Go on. No time to waste.'

'Are you sure? I mean...'

'Chris, I brought up two little girls. You've met one of them. See what you can do for that poor woman and her baby.'

'Is that all right with you, Molly?'

'Yes,' said Molly, grinning all over her face. She threw the dice again. 'You've got to miss a go, Daddy.'

'You're telling me.' He dropped a quick kiss on her hair. 'Be good.' He looked at Faith. 'See you later. And thanks.'

It was odd. Being in Chris's house with his daughter, but without him. They finished the game, then Molly said, 'Can we start my garden?'

'We can plan it, sweetheart. And we can walk across to my house now and get a big flower book so you can tell me what you want me to paint.'

Molly was charmed with the gate and went through it several times.

She wanted another look at Faith's garden mural too. But eventually they were back in Chris's cottage.

Faith had told Chris the truth. She'd felt perfectly confident that she could look after Molly. For a start, the two of them were now firm friends and she had the experience of bringing up younger sisters.

But it wasn't the same. With Hope and Charity, no matter what authority she thought she had, she was still ultimately their sister. With Molly it was different. The child was so much younger that it felt more as if she was a ... mother? And being a mother felt strange and different and rather nice. But to be Molly's mother she would have to be married to Chris. That was definitely a thought too far.

'Let's look at the pictures and you can decide which you like,' she said to her little charge. 'And then it's bathtime and bed.'

'And a story?'

'Of course,' said Faith.

The evening couldn't have gone better. Two stories were needed instead of one, but that was no hardship. Faith sat by Molly's bed, watched her go to sleep. Molly was becoming a different child from the spoiled, scared, slightly wild creature she had been when they had first met. Country life and a settled routine suited her.

Faith switched on the child alarm and went downstairs to sit comfortably on the couch and sketch gardens. It was oddly painful at first, memories of when she'd done it last kept intruding and she had to wait until her eyes cleared. But she persevered, became engrossed and the first indication she had of Chris's return was when she heard the front door quietly open and shut. One look at his face told her all she needed to know.

What to do? What did she want at a time like this? She crossed to him, put her arms round him and hugged him sympathetically. Then she said, 'Molly and I had a lovely time. Why don't you go up and see her for a minute. I'll make you a mug of tea. I could do a quick omelette too if you like?'

He still hadn't spoken. Now he said, 'Sounds like a good idea. Faith, we did what we could but...'

'I know,' she said. 'You don't have to tell me, I've been there myself and I know what it's like. You know there's nothing more you could have done but you feel a failure. But that was then and this is now. Go and kiss your daughter goodnight.'

So he went upstairs. When he came down again she had hot food and drink waiting for him. He ate mechanically, then leant back with his eyes closed and pain etched into his face. She left it to him to speak. She knew he would eventually, there were always feelings that needed to be brought out into the open after a bad operation. She sat by his side, intending to sketch some more. But the failure rolling off him was too much for her to bear. She wrapped her hand gently around his. Slowly she felt some of the tension leaving him.

'She'd lost too much blood,' he said in an exhausted voice. 'There was massive trauma to the chest, a fractured skull. Abdomen messed up too ... it must have been a hell of a crash. She was only twenty-five, a young, strong woman and she hung on for longer than I would have thought possible. But although we all worked as best we could, we knew there could only be one ending. I got the baby out. Not a real Caesarean, half the cutting had already been done by torn metal in the car. I got the baby to the paediatric team – it was a little boy. But too much damage had already been done. He died after half an hour.'

'Any relatives there?'

'The husband. I had to talk to him. That's never a job that is easy. Then I left him with Jared Carpenter while I dealt with the paperwork.' For a moment Chris's mask of despair lifted. 'Jared was far better at dealing with the husband than I expected. Better than I was, I think. Straight into the counselling, if any of it sticks through the poor bloke's shock. That lad has got everything it takes to be a great doctor. Oh, God, Faith, I feel lousy.'

'I know.'

'Why did you send me up to look at Molly?'

'Silly. To be reminded that there is life as well as death.'

'Clever, aren't you? How did your evening go?'

She knew what he was doing, he was trying to find a way back to normality, trying to anchor himself in the ordinary, the simple good things in life. 'Well, I'm afraid you did appallingly in the game once Molly was in charge of your moves. But we fetched a flower book to look at and she decided she wants a big tree painted around her wardrobe. And she told me all about the fairies. My word, there are a lot of them.'

Chris gave a faint smile. 'A whole series. I'll have you know those fairies are all close personal friends to me by now. Are they going to feature in the painting?'

'Heavily, it seems. I'll have to practise.' She could tell by his gradual relaxation that things were becoming easier in his head now. She glanced at her watch, nearly midnight. 'Time I was going. I've got a full day tomorrow.'

'You always have a full day. I'm sorry you have to go. It's so nice sitting next to someone comfortable and understanding and non-critical.' He turned his head, 'Thank you, Faith.'

She didn't kid herself that he meant playing with Molly and rustling him up an omelette. 'You'd do the same for me, for any of the team.'

The team. There she went again, pretending that they were just colleagues.

He held her eyes for a moment, then got up. 'I'll walk you back.'

He switched on the outside light so it illuminated his garden; she could see the new little gate. And there was her kitchen light. She shook her head. 'There's no need, Chris. I'm practically home already. You've made it easy.'

She had intended just to brush his cheek with her lips. This evening there had been too much emotion already. But the fraction of a second when he turned his head was enough to change everything. His cheek was slightly rough, he had not shaved since the morning. There was the faint touch of citrus aftershave and it was warmed by the scent of his skin. A warm, exciting, essentially male combination.

Chris made a tiny sound. Of pain? Of pleasure? Then somehow his arms had slid round her waist to hold her securely and she was holding him too. She felt a great sense that ... that everything was proper. This was like coming home, this was where she belonged. He was so gentle. The knowledge was there in her head that if she wanted she could stop this kiss, could step back, smile, and say goodnight. And because she felt so certain ... why, she might as well stay where she was. She hadn't realised how much she'd missed this closeness to a man. It was glorious.

She held him a little more firmly. Their bodies were pressed together, she felt his thigh next to hers, her breasts squeezed against the muscles of his chest. And she liked it. Her arm wrapped itself round his neck. She was pulling him closer to her, her mouth opening to accept him. She was swept away by her need and by his. The embrace was happening without any planning, any thought, but it all seemed to be so right. It was right. She could feel the strength of his desire for her, but for the moment she didn't care. She was being kissed, she was enjoying it, she wanted...

What was she doing! She hadn't intended this. Faith pulled her arm from round his neck and broke off the kiss. She moved away, looking at Chris with consternation.

He had released her at once. But she could feel the regret. 'Oh, God, Faith,' he said, his voice shaking. He carried on just as if she had spoken aloud. 'I'm so sorry. Wrong time, wrong reason. But don't think I didn't want to go on.'

So had she. It was profoundly disturbing.

She made herself speak. 'I ... I don't know what to say. It was lovely, but...'

Chris shook his head helplessly. 'I know. I know. Oh why do I always mess up?'

'You don't,' Faith said quickly. She put her hand back on his arm. 'Chris, you really don't. Like you said, it was just the wrong time and for the wrong reason. But that doesn't mean to say it was wrong completely.'

He looked at her, but she couldn't read his expression. 'Really?'

And now she was uncertain again. 'Really. You didn't mess up. I didn't mind. I ... I need to think things through. I'll see you tomorrow.'

Wrong time, wrong reason. As she walked back with her thoughts in turmoil and the taste of him on her lips, she wondered if she would ever be brave enough for the right time and the right reason.

The next day Faith went into town during

her lunch hour and bought a selection of art materials. This was going to be hard, but it would be a new start and she could do it. Molly was to move to the little bedroom while her walls were painted, but Faith promised she'd be as fast as she could.

'I like watching,' said Molly, and truth to tell, it was only the fact that the little girl was there, chattering away and playing games with Panda and her other toys, that got Faith through that first day.

She'd known it was going to be difficult getting back into painting, but she hadn't fully realised how horribly painful this particular process was going to be. Reproducing her and Mike's garden mural was bringing her happiness with him – and her devastation after he died – so powerfully to mind that she could barely function.

She started with a wash of sky. That was easy, it could have been just pale blue painted walls. The first blades of grass weren't too bad. The rose bush was when she started to falter, remembering Mike fooling around and pretending to catch himself on the thorns, remembering him really stabbing himself when he brought a long stem inside for her to copy.

Molly bounced on the dust-sheeted bed.

'Now do Fairy Rose.'

Faith pulled herself back to the present. 'Pardon?'

'Fairy Rose. That's where she lives.' Molly rolled off the bed and ran downstairs for her story book, completely confident that Faith could reproduce the character.

'Oh,' said Faith a little blankly. 'All right.'

The next two days were similar. Whenever Faith's memories threatened to get the upper hand, Molly's input into the garden frieze – along with the addition of several fairies who were apparently too impatient to wait for their new home to be finished before moving in – brought her back to earth. As was fitting, the mural was becoming much more her young client's than hers.

'Do the tree next,' said Molly, just as Faith was finishing for the night. 'I want it to be my cave.'

Faith wrinkled her brow. 'It's only a painting, darling.'

'That's all you know,' said Chris, who had come upstairs with coffee. 'She likes curling up in wardrobes. Had you not noticed that none of the cupboard doors are closed in this house?'

'Of course I had. I assumed you were both untidy.'

He grinned at her. 'I suspect Molly's wardrobe is destined to be a hollow tree like Fairy Maple's. I'll have to find somewhere else for her clothes to live.'

Faith smiled back. 'That's your problem. I'll do the tree tomorrow. I'm sure Molly will tell me if I go wrong.'

But tomorrow, it transpired, Molly was going to Hannah's birthday party. 'Don't do the tree until I get back,' she said.

'All right, darling. I'll paint some more flowers instead. Don't you look nice in your fairy dress!'

'Yes, and I can twirl in it,' said Molly, doing so. 'It's got a big bow at the back that Daddy had to tie.'

The cottage was strangely quiet with them gone. Faith painted a stand of poppies, then started on a hollyhock. Part of her noticed that without Molly here, she was painting in a more detailed manner, more as she had done at home with Mike. A tear fell on her hand. Faith looked at it and realised she was crying. Faith painted another foot of hollyhock before her tears blinded her.

'Faith?' That was Chris's voice, back from dropping Molly at the party.

She kept her back turned. 'Yes?'

'Faith, what's the matter?'

Perhaps even then she would have held out except she felt his hand on her arm, his voice concerned.

'Faith? Faith, what's the matter? Tell me?'

And suddenly, she couldn't hold back any more. 'Mike,' she said.

Chris took the paintbrush out of her hand, drew her over to the bed and sat her down next to him. 'Tell me?' he said simply.

It was almost a relief that he had asked. This was her story – her life. 'Nobody has mentioned it?'

He shook his head. 'People have hinted. I could have pressed, but I haven't. I'd rather hear it from you.' He rubbed his thumb across her fingers. 'It's going to hurt, isn't it? I'm sorry.'

'Yes, it hurts. Because it was so special while it lasted.' She paused a moment. 'I'm twenty-nine now. You already know about my parents. They looked after the world, rather than us, so I took it on myself to bring my sisters up. Someone had to – I didn't see that I had a choice. That's why I took my first post here, to keep an eye on them. I thought I was going to be the responsible one for ever. But I met Mike Croft almost straight away. He was a local GP and … and *fun.*'

She looked up at Chris, willing him to understand. 'There was me, serious, self-sufficient, more likely to be helping others than needing help myself. And there was Mike, a caring, laughing man who had fallen in love with me.' She shook her head, remembering. 'To have a partner, sharing ideas and emotions and feelings, was so different. We planned our future, we looked at lots of houses before we found Fell View cottage. We decided on the best time to have children – not too soon, because we wanted to enjoy each other – and we chose possible names for them. We planned our decorating so the whole cottage would be harmonised. He encouraged my painting. I encouraged his gardening. And I painted the garden mural in the back scullery – my art room.'

She had to pause, the memories were filling her eyes and throat with tears.

Chris slid his arm round her. After a moment, he said gently, 'So what went wrong?'

'Mike was a member of the Territorial Army. He was sent to Iraq. And was killed there. I got the news of his death two days before my twenty-fifth birthday. On the mantelpiece there were birthday cards and messages of sympathy side by side. It took me a long time to recover from the shock. I put my painting things away, decided to concentrate on my career. No more love. Not for me. Because if love so easily turns into tragedy, why risk it? I couldn't take the pain again.'

Standing there with Faith folded against his chest, holding her safe and close, a great dam of sympathy flooded through Chris. He'd suspected something traumatic in her past, now he knew. Part of him wanted to applaud her for keeping her lover's memory alight. Part of him wanted to reassure her over and over again that life went on, it had to. And part of him... Chris suddenly went cold and ashamed as he realised. Part of him was prickling with jealousy that she had loved this man with her whole heart. A man who wasn't him.

'And now?' he murmured. 'Do you still believe in no more love?'

'I don't know. I just don't know.'

She was so lovely in his arms. He wanted to keep her there. 'Faith, I really want to kiss you again, but I don't know whether that's a good idea or a bad idea.'

She was still for a few moments more. Then she sighed. 'If you don't know, then it's probably a bad idea, Chris.'

She pulled back. Reluctantly, he let her go. She was right. He suspected if they had kissed, things would have gone a lot further than either of them intended. And after that, he wouldn't be able to give her up, which would be potentially appalling for his daughter's recovery.

Surprisingly, it was Molly herself who took the next step. She came home full of the party, telling them all about it and wanting to go to another one very, very soon. Her own, preferably.

Chris smiled. 'Sweetheart, it's not your birthday for another three months.'

Once she had an idea in her mind, Molly tended not to let it go. 'You have a birthday party, then.'

'My birthday's after Christmas – that's even longer.'

'What about Faith?'

As Chris watched, Faith's hand clenched, then relaxed. 'Oh, I don't make a fuss of birthdays any more.'

'But did you used to?'

'Yes, darling. Just not any more.' Faith seemed to be making an effort to talk normally. With a flash of insight, Chris realised why. Her birthday would remind her of

Mike's death, of course. He ached with sympathy for her.

'But they're nice! I like parties. There's going to be a picnic soon that Abbey says is like a party. With food and paddling and games. And mummies or daddies have to come too.'

Faith smiled. 'The Little Allaby picnic down by the river? They have that every year. It always looks fun.'

'Abbey says it's *mega* fun.' Molly smiled sunnily up at her. 'You can come with Daddy and me.'

Chris saw Faith catch her breath. 'But–'

He spoke quickly. 'That would be lovely. Will you, Faith?'

'I...' Her eyes connected with his, uncertain but not, he thought, unwilling. 'Yes,' she said. 'Yes, I'd like that. Thank you.'

'This picnic tomorrow,' said Chris, catching Faith after the briefing on Friday. 'Is the river safe?'

Faith smiled. He was a typical father. 'Perfectly,' she reassured him. 'It's wide and shallow and very slow moving. People often paddle and swim in it during the summer. I'm surprised you haven't seen them. You and Molly must have been across the bridge

174

there masses of times.'

He gave her a dry look. 'Seeing other people messing about in the water is a totally different thing from letting my own child go paddling. I'll fish out her swimming costume and a towel.'

'And a dry change,' suggested Faith, remembering previous years. 'From what I gather, at least one child falls into the water fully dressed every year. Apart from that, they just wear clothes for playing on a river bank. Shorts, t-shirts and a sun hat.'

'Will you be wearing shorts too?'

Faith eyed him suspiciously. 'Probably. Why?'

He looked blandly back. 'So I know to fit in, of course.'

He was as good as his word. Chris opened the door to her on Saturday morning in a crisp white t-shirt and dark blue shorts. *Wow*, she thought, trying not to stare. She cleared her throat. 'Ready?'

He gestured to a rucksack and cold box. 'We've been ready for hours. Molly only just let dawn break before she was nagging at me to start making sandwiches.'

Faith chuckled, took the hand that the little girl slipped into hers and they set off down the road and over the bridge. *Almost like being a family*, she thought to herself. And then had to swallow down the lump in her throat and pretend she'd got an eyelash in her eye.

It wasn't very far, just over the bridge to where a grassy bank in a wide half-circle made a perfect picnic spot, with a tiny beach edging a shallow part of the river.

Abbey and Jack Kirk were already there, along with several other parents, watching a handful of children paddling and splashing in the water. 'There's Hannah,' Molly shouted, 'and Peter and Joseph. They're my friends. Can I go in the water as well?'

'As soon as we get your costume on,' Chris said.

The mums were from the village, Faith knew them all. There might have been questions in the air as people saw her walk down with Chris and Molly, but this was Little Appleby. They accepted her for herself just as they accepted Chris as a single parent.

It was a good picnic. Lots of splashing, lots of screaming and of course some inevitable tears. Faith had decided not to bring her costume, but since she was in shorts she went for a paddle with Molly while Chris chatted with the parents. Naturally, she was splashed too. Then she dried off in the sun and it was Chris's turn to get wet.

Surrounded by all the village families, the solid lump of longing in Faith's chest grew heavier.

'I do like crusts a bit now,' Molly told her when the children were finally called out of the water for their picnic lunch. 'Everybody else eats them.'

'Seems a good reason to me,' said Faith. She unwrapped a foil package and smiled at the precise triangles of cheese and cucumber sandwich.

Chris's eyes met hers. 'I can't help it,' he said ruefully. 'I have *tried* to make a messy sandwich but I just can't bring myself to.'

'Shh,' said Faith. 'I love them exactly as they are.'

After lunch, it was time to get dressed and explore. There were woods by the river, and through them ran a path to a tiny quarry known to have shiny stones in it. Diamonds, perhaps? Faith and Chris set off with the others, Molly swinging between them.

'This is nice,' said Chris quietly. His green gaze connected with Faith. 'Is it nice for you too? You're not regretting taking a day off from painting Molly's bedroom?'

Around them were conversations, trees,

clean air, blue sky, children's voices and a village that she'd made her home in. Between them was a happy little girl. 'I'm having a nice time too,' she said, and she tried to ignore the fact that the little girl wasn't hers and that both she and Chris were encased in old pain.

Just next to the path was an ancient oak tree with a thick trunk that was completely hollow inside. It was evidently well known to the older village children who each ducked inside and then out again before running off down the path. Molly was entranced. She went in and sat down, looking around in wonder.

'It's Fairy Maple's tree,' she breathed. 'It really is. Just like in the story.'

'It's *like* her tree,' said Faith, 'but it isn't *actually* her tree.'

Molly gave no sign of having heard her. 'But there are no fairies here.'

'Perhaps they've gone to play with their friends,' said Chris. 'Just as we're going to do. Come on, sweetheart.'

Molly wriggled further inside. 'Going to stay here.'

Faith saw Chris's body tense up. 'You can't,' he said, still in a reasonable tone. 'We're all going to look for shiny stones, then there are going to be races.'

Molly's mouth set in a mulish line. 'Want to stay here!'

Faith sighed. 'Well, you *can*, of course, but I don't think there will be any tea here, and it's going to be really difficult for us to tell Panda and the other toys that you aren't in bed for them to cuddle up to tonight because you are sitting down here in a tree in the cold and the dark.'

Molly mulled this over. Then she sighed too. 'Oh all right,' she said in a long-suffering voice that had Faith biting her cheeks not to laugh. She came out of the tree and took a hand each of Faith and Chris again.

Faith darted a sideways look at Chris as they followed the others. His eyes were brimming with laughter. He made a strangled sound, shaking his head to stop her speaking. Faith bit her cheeks even harder to keep the laughter in.

In the 'quarry' they found a few stones with just enough sparkle to keep Molly happy, then it was back to the riverbank for races, and finally time to go home.

They arrived back at Chris's cottage. 'Aren't you coming in too?' said Molly, giving a huge yawn.

Faith looked down at the little girl and

smiled. 'I don't think I'd better. You need a nap and I've got a chicken casserole to make for my dinner.'

'I like your cooking,' said Molly with another yawn.

'A casserole sounds wonderful,' agreed Chris. Both of them looked at her hopefully.

'I *could* bring it over when it's cooked,' she said, but hesitantly, in case that hadn't been Chris's idea at all.

'Yes, please,' he said, barely giving her time to finish the sentence. 'I'll provide the wine to drink with it.'

'See you in a couple of hours, then,' she said, her heart warming. It had been a lovely day, one she didn't want to end.

Chris opened the front door and went inside, almost as tired as Molly, but with a small undercurrent of excitement running through him. It had been lovely, spending time out with Faith. Almost like being a...

No! Don't say the word!

But his head supplied it anyway. *Family*.

'Read me Fairy Maple's story, Daddy? Now?'

He might have guessed, after her finding that tree. But looking at her heavy eyelids, he suspected he wouldn't be reading to the end. An hour's nap would do her the world of good. 'All right, sweetheart,' he said. 'Cuddle up here with Panda.'

As he expected, her eyes were shut within minutes. He lifted her gently on to her squashy beanbag and tucked Panda next to her. And now he would make a strong coffee and work like a madman on accumulated paperwork to give him the rest of the weekend free.

It was an email, pinging into his inbox, that made him realise the hour was up. He should be rousing Molly or she wouldn't sleep that night. 'Wake up, sleepyhead,' he said, going into the living room.

It was empty.

Upstairs, he thought, in her wardrobe-version of the tree. But she wasn't there either. Chris's heart stuttered as he took in the empty room. 'Molly,' he shouted, 'Molly where are you?' He raced into every room, looking in cupboards and under beds. He hurtled down the stairs three at a time. 'Molly!' he yelled. 'Molly, where are you?'

No answer. Molly wasn't in the house.

Panicking now, he snatched up his phone and dialled Faith. 'Is Molly with you?'

She sounded startled. 'No. I haven't seen her since I got home.'

'Can you check all through your house? She might have crept in.'

He heard her breathing speed up and the sound of rapid footsteps as she ran from room to room. 'I'm looking. But I've been in the kitchen all afternoon. She would have had to get past me. There's no sign, Chris.'

'She fell asleep reading a story, so I put her on the beanbag and blitzed those damn reports from yesterday. But now she isn't here! Not anywhere.'

'Wardrobe? Any other cubby holes? I'll try my shed.' She was still running, her footsteps thudding.

'I've looked! I'll try in the outhouse.' For the life of him he couldn't keep his voice from shaking. Where was she?

'She's not here, Chris. I'm coming over.' Her voice was as anxious as his.

He fumbled with the back door, still gripping the phone. It was locked. Molly couldn't have got out that way. He went outside anyway. The outhouse was empty.

Faith came racing up the garden and through the gate, looking as frantic as he felt. 'Two pairs of eyes are better than one,' she said.

'Molly,' she called, going into the house. 'It's me – Faith.'

Chris halted in the living room, his fists balled with frustration. And realised something else was missing. 'She's taken Panda,' he said.

Faith reappeared in the doorway. 'Exploring?' she asked. Then her hands flew to her mouth. 'Chris! The tree in the park! But it's impossible. How would she have got out?'

'She couldn't. The back door was locked and I always bolt the front... Oh my God...' Because he hadn't. He'd been tired and thinking about Faith and he'd just come straight in. He pushed past Faith to check. The front door was ajar. 'Oh my God!'

Faith grabbed his hand. 'Come on,' she gasped. She pulled him outside and started to run.

'Village shop,' Chris panted. 'Someone might have seen her.'

'If they had, they'd have brought her back or rung you to fetch her,' said Faith, not slowing down. 'That's how the village works. But everyone will have left the river by now, so they might not see her looking for "Fairy Maple's tree". That's got to be where she is.' Her voice wavered. 'If she's found the way.'

The river! Dear heaven! Chris caught up with Faith in less than a second, gripping her hand, neither of them letting up their speed.

Over the bridge, their footsteps pounding in unison. Faith wheeled sharply right. Chris swept the riverbank and tiny beach a cursory glance but there was no little girl, no bright pink panda. He faltered, looking at the river itself, but Faith tugged him on.

His heart was beating more thunderously than it had done in months. A very faint part of him knew lots of children wandered off with no harm coming to them. But to some children it did. What if Molly was injured in the village somewhere while he was off on a wild goose chase in the woods? What if something worse had happened?

'Watch your step,' panted Faith. She'd let go of him and was flying between bushes, snapping twigs and skidding on loose earth. She tripped, fell headlong and fetched up against the tree. She flapped her hand at him, too winded to speak.

Chris raced around and there, calm and still inside the hollow, sat Molly and Panda. 'Sweetheart,' he said, slumping to the ground. 'Don't you ever, ever do that to me again.' He reached for her, tears running down his face.

'There's still no fairies here,' Molly said in

a disappointed voice. 'I wanted to bring Panda to see them. We were going to come back for you when you'd finished your work.'

Chapter Eight

Oh please, prayed Faith as Chris rounded the tree. *Please let Molly be there.* Her prayer was answered as Chris drew his daughter out for a much-needed cuddle. Faith held onto the rough bark of the tree and waited for her fast-beating heart to slow down. Emotions surged through her. Thankfulness, gratitude, an immense desire to shake Molly for giving her a fright, but a much stronger one to hug her hard because it had been borne into her with the impact of a sledgehammer that the child meant so, so much to her.

She lurched upright, wrapping her arms around both Molly and Chris. 'We thought you were lost,' she said. 'Please don't ever do that again without telling someone where you're going.'

Two fat tears trickled down Molly's face. 'I

only wanted to see Fairy Maple.'

'Yes, sweetheart, but we didn't know that and we were worried,' said Chris.

'But you were busy and Faith was at her house and...' Molly paused. 'I'm hungry,' she said, with the air of making a discovery.

'Good,' said Faith. 'Because I have a casserole in the oven just waiting to be eaten.'

'And I have wine just waiting to be drunk,' murmured Chris. 'And boy, do I need it.' His hand touched Faith's arm as she stepped back from the group hug. 'Thank you.'

'And can Faith stay and do my bath and read me a story?'

Faith looked at Chris. His deep green eyes looked back steadily. 'She can stay as long as she likes,' he said.

Did that mean...? Faith ducked her head and concentrated on walking back to the bridge without losing her footing again.

Back at home, she stripped off the t-shirt and shorts she'd been wearing all day and had a rapid shower. What to wear now, though? After considering half the contents of her wardrobe, Faith picked loose, dark blue trousers and a light blue silk blouse and laid them on the bed. She pulled open her underwear drawer. Nestling at the back were two sets Hope had brought her last Christmas, so far unworn. Pink lacy satin and cream lacy satin. *Underwear to be seen*, Hope had said with a meaningful look. *Seen by a man*, she had added, in case her meaning wasn't clear. Of course, she hadn't been in her foreswearing-men phase then.

Faith didn't think things were going to go anywhere near that far, but she picked up the lacy cream set anyway.

Then she stood – still, silent and naked. Because just in case events did move in that direction, she should be prepared. She had lost count of the number of times she'd advised women never to rely on the man. She pulled out the bottom drawer of her bedside cabinet, felt around and took out a tube of cream, a small circular plastic container. It was a very long time since she had needed either.

Her pulse was beating fast as she walked down her garden, through the gate and up towards Chris's cottage carefully bearing her casserole. As he opened the door, she realised he had changed too, into dark trousers and a white shirt. He looked wonderful.

As it was still warm, Chris had moved the table and chairs out from the conservatory to the patio. They had Faith's food with lovely crusty rolls to soak up the gravy.

Chris poured two glasses of a full-bodied red wine, with orange juice for Molly. Then there was ice-cream for afterwards, a splashy bath time, two stories – one read by each of them – and finally the little girl was tucked up fast asleep in bed, the scare of the afternoon over, full of a lovely day to dream about instead.

Chris bent over, touched her forehead gently with his lips and ushered Faith back downstairs. On the patio again with dusk falling, he refilled their glasses, sipped from his and said, 'All the things that have gone wrong over the last five years, the bitterness, the despair – all the times I've known I was failing … but she's worth it. I swear my heart stopped this afternoon when I couldn't find her.'

'You're lucky.' Faith turned her head as if studying the plants in the border, tears stinging her eyes.

'I didn't feel lucky for a long time, but yes, even through all the anger, guilt and sheer helplessness, it's the one thing I've always hung on to. Lorraine and I got married in haste. We were in love. We thought we knew each other, but we didn't. She didn't ever try to understand how I felt about my work, my department. And even though I tried to be around for her as much as I could, I often failed. There were arguments all the time, accusations... But then I think of Molly and I know those years weren't wasted.'

Faith gave a painful laugh. 'Whereas Mike and I never argued once. We didn't have a moment that wasn't pure happiness. We planned and planned and never thought of the unexpected. So when he was torn away I had nothing left at all.'

'You have your memories of his love. There's nothing to plague *your* dreams.'

'But I have nothing of *him*,' she whispered, feeling that chasm of emptiness again.

'Oh, Faith.' Chris caught her movement of distress and put his hand on hers.

She turned towards him blindly.

His arms came around her, his mouth covered hers, easing the desolation. It started out as nothing more than a kiss of comfort, but as she shifted her body to fit more comfortably against his, it changed. There was a raw need in both of them. Their lips locked, their hearts pounded so hard that Faith could feel the beat of Chris's against her own ribs.

Not just his heart either. Chris was holding her so tightly she could feel all of him, his arms, his chest, his legs. One hand cupped her neck, kept her pressed against him so their lips met with a searing mutual desire. She matched his caresses with a passion that startled her. *Make love to me, Chris? Now. Please?* Had she said it aloud?

After long, long moments, his hold relaxed. His hands slipped down her body, held her lightly round her waist. He took his lips from hers, his breathing ragged. 'I know what I want,' he said. 'And it's not just now, not just because of the picnic and the sunshine and the panic and the meal together and the wine. This has been building for a long time. But it has to be an equal decision.'

'I do want it.' And she did, or at least she had wanted it two minutes ago. But now, with him asking, she could see everything they were heading towards draining away. The excitement, apprehension, the burgeoning something inside her was making her uncertain. She was absolutely sure making love with Chris would be wonderful. But she also knew her life would never be the same afterwards.

'You're thinking,' he said softly. 'Sweetheart, you aren't worried, are you? Because if you are, we'll stop.'

'No. I've never been so certain in my life. I'm just thinking that after tonight everything will be different. But I'm looking forward to it.'

'I feel the same way. If you close your eyes I could kiss your eyelids.'

She closed them. 'That sounds nice.'

He kissed her eyelids and it was lovely. Everything was lovely, especially where his hands were roaming now. She felt him undo her top button, then the next and the next. The warm evening air caressed her exposed skin. His hands slid over the mound of her breast, causing her legs to tremble.

They moved wordlessly inside and up the stairs, Faith's fingers working on Chris's shirt buttons just as he was working on hers. As they reached his bedroom, her blouse fell away. She felt a wriggle of pleasure at the way his eyes gleamed and his mouth curved into a smile.

'That is one beautiful bra,' he murmured.

'Hope gave it to me for Christmas. She said it was underwear to be seen.'

'Smart girl, your sister. Am I allowed to do anything more than just look at it?'

His fingers were already sliding around the lace, investigating the slinky straps. Faith experienced an erotic sense of power. 'We-ell,' she said. 'I suppose you could also take it off – if you like.'

'Oh, I do like. I like very much.' His hands went round her back, skilled surgeon's fingers had no difficulty in unfastening the bra clasp. He dropped it carefully onto her blouse. Chris bent his head and took her breast into his mouth and ... and ... this was heaven! Time stood still as she arched her back in pleasure, enjoying sensations that had been missing from her life for so long.

His mouth moved up to hers again. Her hands trembled as she stripped off his shirt. His chest was muscular, covered with a sprinkling of dark hairs. His skin brushing hers seemed to burn her with delight. Her breasts felt full, her nipples stiff with excitement, rubbing against him.

He kissed her again, demanding, insistent, his tongue seeking out the softness of the inside of her mouth. She clutched at him, pulled all of him to her, was suddenly, intoxicatingly aware of his need for her and of her need for him. Her heart was thudding in her chest, this was what she wanted.

He broke off, dazed and reluctant. 'Faith, this is awkward. I wasn't expecting this. I haven't got any ... that is we can't...'

She recaptured his mouth. 'Yes, we can. I didn't *expect* – but I did take precautions. Just in case.'

His fingers stroked down her sides, slipped forward and loosened her belt then eased down her trousers. He knelt, letting his fingers trail down her legs, and it felt magic. One by one he took off her shoes leaving her in just the lacy cream knickers. He slid his fingers up her legs again, over the silken scrap of material, hooked his thumbs in the elastic... Faith sighed with pure pleasure as he slipped the panties off.

She was naked and she was happy. He stepped back a little, looked at her and she thrilled at the desire in his eyes. 'You're still a touch overdressed,' she murmured. Her hands went to his belt.

She heard an indrawn breath, felt his abdominal muscles tighten. 'Sweetheart, if you take too long over that I'm going to disgrace myself,' he said. Before she knew what was happening he had lifted her across to his bed and laid her on it, his hands lingering appreciatively on her waist and hips. How had he done that so easily? Faith hadn't realised Chris was so strong!

And then he was lying next to her, as naked as she, and as evidently aroused by her nearness as she was by his.

She stretched luxuriously, heady with happiness. He stroked her arms from fingertips down to shoulders. 'Just lie like that for a moment. Faith, this is so wonderful that I can't believe it is happening to me.'

'It's not just happening to you. It's happening to us.' She felt she was in another world. The past, the future had disappeared. There was only the now, and she was wondrously, wondrously happy. And she knew soon she would be happier still. Because he was going to...

There were only so many places on her face that he could kiss. But he somehow kissed them all, his hands exploring her body at the same time. When she tried to reciprocate, he gently lifted her arms back out of the way. 'Not finished yet,' he murmured wickedly.

So she surrendered. And realised through her haze of pleasure that this was something that he was doing not only *to* her, but *for* her, almost an act of worship. She arched lustfully, thinking she would let him for now – and then she would do the same for him later.

The kisses didn't stop at her face. His lips roamed down her neck, across her shoulders onto her breasts. And then she heard herself moaning with pleasure as he took each proud nipple into his mouth, stroked it gently with his tongue. So much delight!

Could there be more? But then his head moved even lower and she had to grip her hands together as his flickering tongue brought her to an ecstasy she had forgotten.

After she gasped with incoherent joy she took hold of his shoulders. 'Enough, Chris, please. My turn.'

His body was magnificent. Muscled, toned, not an ounce of fat on him. But as sensitive as hers. She kissed him greedily in all the places he had kissed her. And she rejoiced in his reactions. She had never really appreciated that a man's nipples could be as sensitive as hers. Apparently, they were. But when she went even lower, took him into her mouth, he first arched then gasped.

'Too much,' he said. 'Much too much. Another time, sweetheart. Come back up here. There's something far more important I want us to do together right now.'

She knew. She could feel it in him and in herself. He pulled her up to lie on top of him, kissing her for a endless, soul-jolting moment. Then he rolled them both over so that he was on top. They were moving towards a culmination, a crescendo of mutual need that couldn't be postponed for much longer.

He slid inside her and it was a moment of

joy, like coming home. This was meant to be. She clutched him, moved with him, murmured his name as sensations of glory travelled around her body. She gripped harder, urged him onwards so that he too would share in that moment of ecstasy that was so close, so close, so close... 'Chris,' she screamed, 'oh Chris...'

'Faith,' he said. 'Faith, Faith, Faith, Faith, Faith.' There was a groan, a sob of happiness.

And then it was over.

This was true happiness, Chris thought drowsily. He was as content as he had ever been in his life. Faith was asleep. She lay in his arms, cradled against his chest. He could feel the warmth of her breath on his skin. He didn't want to wake her, but just for a moment, very gently, he stroked his fingertips down her naked back. She was wonderful. He was the luckiest man in the world.

Chapter Nine

It was early morning, just getting light. Faith woke with an enormous sense of happiness. She was in bed with Chris, he had made love to her ... no, they had made love to each other. And it had been wonderful. She lay for a moment, perfectly still, realising that she'd finally allowed herself to love again, to take that risk.

She turned her head to look at him. He was still fast asleep. There was a half smile on his lips, his face looked relaxed, younger. He looked ... vulnerable.

She was lying on her back, he was on his side facing her, his hand resting lightly on her hip. She had lovely half-waking, half-sleeping memories of the night they had just spent together. They both seemed to have been determined not to let go of the other. When he had turned his back to her, she had nestled close to him, her arm round him, her knees behind his, her breasts touching the muscles of his back. When she had turned, he had done the same. It had

197

been good.

But ... she was going to have to get up. Gather her clothes and go back home. She didn't want to.

She kissed his forehead. 'Chris, I should go.'

'Mmm?' He nuzzled closer, kissed her shoulder. It felt warm, safe, dangerously enticing.

'I hate to say this, but I should go. I don't know what time Molly wakes, but–'

His eyes flew open. 'Molly! You're right. She mustn't find you here! God knows what it would do to her psyche.'

Faith felt a tiny, tiny stab that he was more concerned about Molly than about her. 'That's why I'm going,' she said, telling herself not to be ridiculous. 'I should be in different clothes the next time I see her.'

Chris cupped her cheek, his expression remorseful. 'You know I don't want you to.'

'I don't either, but there's no sense in rushing her. We'll just take things slowly.'

'Faith, you don't quite understand. The child psychologist said I shouldn't form a new relationship at all. He said Molly needs a long period of stability.'

His skin against hers was still warm, still lovely, but Faith felt suddenly cold. 'Are you saying that was just a one-night stand?'

'No! Far from it! How could you even think that? But we can't be *seen* to be lovers.'

She met his eyes levelly. 'If you think I am going to make a regular practice of sneaking out of your house in the early hours like a character from a bad farce, you have got another think coming. Chris, your daughter likes me. I certainly love her. She has calmed down so much from when you first moved here. How many tantrums has she had recently? None that I know of since I've been painting her mural.'

'I can't...' He lay back, one hand clutching his hair. 'Faith, I can't risk it.'

Faith raised herself on one elbow, kissed him hard and then slid swiftly out of the bed before she changed her mind. 'I was determined never to get involved with anyone again after Mike because I thought I couldn't take the risk of getting hurt. But I have. I've fallen for you. Giving you up now would be all the pain I didn't want. I really don't think Molly will be a problem if we take things gently with her. If you are reluctant about our relationship – any relationship – maybe you need to look closer to home. You went though hell with Lorraine – are you sure the problem now isn't with *you* not your daughter?'

He stared at her in shock as she dressed. She didn't waver. 'I'll see you later,' she said. 'If you still want me to come over, that is. There's only another day or so to do on the mural before it's finished. Let me know.'

She didn't look back as she let herself out and walked resolutely from his cottage to hers. It nearly killed her to leave him with such a look of anguish on his face, but she was feeling horribly vulnerable too. She'd broken her own rule, given her heart away again, laid herself open to the possibility of pain. If this all went wrong, the emotional fall-out didn't bear thinking about. Chris had to work his demons out for himself.

Chris listened to Faith heading rapidly down the stairs, heard her let herself out, pictured her crossing both gardens and unlocking her back door.

Closer to home.

Lorraine had never lived here, but suddenly the bedroom was full of his ex-wife's presence. Baleful silences. Unfair accusations. Endless, pointless, cyclic arguments with neither of them able to reach the other. He'd been at his wits' end. Sometimes Lorraine didn't seem to have moved at all between him going out in the morning and returning at night. At other times her moods would shift by the minute.

And Molly – Molly had been fussed over, hugged, screamed at, ignored. It was no wonder she'd subsequently played up herself.

But his wife had known, deep down, that she needed help. That was the tragedy, that she'd known and wouldn't let herself admit it. When she'd finally agreed to counselling, Chris had thought they'd turned a corner. Slowly, so slowly, she'd improved. She'd started caring about her appearance again, spent time with Molly. But not with him. She blamed him for her illness, focussed all her feelings of unworthiness and low self-esteem on him, because he had kept going when she hadn't. So she didn't want to see him. And as the improvement in her health continued, she didn't want to see Molly any more either.

Chris sat up, putting his head in his hands. It was full daylight, he realised. The sun had strengthened in the sky while he'd been reliving the nightmare. Could he risk going through that again with another woman? Could he risk compromising Molly's safety a second time?

But, he realised slowly, listening to the small sounds of Molly waking up in the next room, he *hadn't* compromised it the first time. As soon as he recognised that Lorraine's illness was causing her to neglect their small daughter, he'd booked Molly in at a day nursery, dropping her off and collecting her himself. When he saw how upset Molly was by her mother shouting and screaming at him, he'd taken her to stay with his parents. Maybe it *had* reinforced Lorraine's poor self-image, but Molly had been cared for.

And – as Faith had said – his little girl was now a different person. A normal five-year-old. Chris was honest enough to admit that most of the improvement was due to a settled routine and Faith's sensible pointers on childcare.

So ... so Faith had been right. It *was* himself he was worried about. His own heart. He had watched a lively, outgoing woman first succumb to depression and then go beyond it, settling to a dull hatred of him. He had promised to stay with her in sickness and in health, but she had rejected him and blamed him for her change. He couldn't bear that again, either on Molly's account, or on his own. On the other hand, was he really going to risk throwing away a second chance of happiness because of the worry that Faith might go the same way as Lorraine? His feelings for Faith were already much stronger than he'd ever felt for his ex-wife. The guilt would be too.

'Come on, Daddy,' said Molly, clambering on to the bed. 'You said we could go and see Fairy Maple's tree after breakfast.'

'Whose tree?'

Molly sighed and corrected herself. 'The tree that looks like Fairy Maple's.'

'Just you and me?' asked Chris with the sense of a momentous step being taken. 'Or shall we ask Faith along too?'

Monday morning and Faith was in temporary charge of Obs & Gynie. It was odd how different it felt compared to when she had done the same job under Freddie. The department felt different, it had purpose. The first thing Chris would do when he got back from his regional meeting would be to ask for a quick report on the morning's activities. The first thing Freddie would have done would have been to order lunch.

Faith looked again at the letter on her desk. She had been invited to an interview for the Hadrian's Wall Obs & Gynie position. It had brought a decision she'd pushed to one side back to the fore. Did she still want to apply? Her head said it would be foolish to back out having got this far. Her heart ... her heart was in a state of enormous indecision. She knew she loved Chris. She might not have said it to his face yet, but her heart knew it perfectly well. She couldn't have gone to bed with him, couldn't have given herself to him so completely, without loving him.

But what of him? Faith thought he did love her in return, but if he couldn't commit, what future did they have? It was five years this week since she'd lost Mike. She'd managed – not well, but adequately – by shutting out emotion, by focussing on her job and her career. She had come to realise in these past weeks that it wasn't quite enough after all. There was no sense of guilt in her, because Mike would want her to move on and be happy. But whatever she had with Chris must be an equal partnership if they were to take it forward. And if it wasn't equal ... well, she'd rather get any new heartbreak over now rather than later.

Faith sighed and put the letter back on her in-tray, hating herself for wanting to keep her options open. She and Chris had agreed yesterday to take things gradually. It was a prosaic, if not very passionate, decision and she had the feeling it was chafing with both of them. Considering she had held herself back for five years, she was surprised at how much she wanted instant action now.

Her phone rang. A call to the delivery suite. A community midwife – one of a number attached to GP practices who all fed into Dale Head hospital – had requested the presence of a doctor. Faith hurried along and was pleased to find that the midwife was her sister, Hope. After dealing with the birth, she hugged her and said, 'Have you got time for lunch?'

'Of course,' said Hope cheerfully. 'I told my patient to time the baby for as near twelve-thirty as possible for that very reason.'

Faith grinned. Hope was very good for her as long as she wasn't trying to interfere.

'So,' said her sister, as they queued up in the canteen. 'How's your lovely boss?'

Faith eyed her cautiously. 'Settling in nicely.'

'And your handsome neighbour?'

'Fitting in very well with the village.'

Hope chuckled. 'Saw you blush. Have you worn my Christmas presents yet?'

Faith felt herself go scarlet. 'Sometimes I cannot believe I brought you up!'

Hope blew her a kiss. 'I'm not going to

pry, but if you'd like some more sexy underwear for your birthday, you only have to ask.'

'Can we talk about something else, please?'

'I'm only trying to help.'

'Please don't,' replied Faith. 'Your version of helping is often very embarrassing.'

'All right, I'll be good. You remember this primagravida that I've got a hunch about?'

'Yes,' said Faith. Her sister was an experienced midwife, and Faith knew midwives in particular often developed a sixth sense about what might be wrong, a sense that had no basis in obvious medical facts. There was nothing official she could put on the reports, but she never discounted them. 'Have you worked out why?'

'No. Can you come out on a visit with me? I've checked with the boss. He says it's okay.'

'Sure. Where and when?'

'First thing Thursday morning at Thwaite Hall farm. Lizzie's booked in for the hospital for the birth, but the farm is up by Yallendale. It's so easy to get cut off up there that I'm doing a home assessment at the same time as her normal check-up just in case.'

Faith was dismayed. She and Chris were both off-duty on Thursday. They'd planned to take Molly out for the day to a woodland adventure playground as another doing-things-together day. 'How early first thing?'

'It's my first appointment.'

'Okay. I'll meet you there.' That wasn't too bad. They'd stop on the way and Chris and Molly could wait in the car or perhaps look at the animals in the farmyard if there were any.

The outing didn't start propitiously. For a start, it was the anniversary of the day that Faith had heard about Mike's death five years ago. Try as she might, she couldn't push aside the memory.

The second reason was Molly. 'You could have asked Hannah to come with us if you'd wanted, to say thank you for her birthday party,' said Chris as they were getting into the car.

Molly's face darkened. 'Hannah's stupid. I hate her.'

Faith and Chris looked at each other in alarm. 'But you were both playing together when I popped in yesterday,' said Faith.

'Yes, but then she said her Mummy said you were going to be my new mummy! And you're not.' Her voice rose. 'Not, not, not! I don't want you to be my mummy. I want you to be my Faith. Hannah's stupid!'

Faith felt a stab of pain in her chest so sharp she nearly doubled over. Chris was looking equally stricken. She couldn't dwell on it though. Molly had dissolved into sobbing tears. 'Hush, darling,' she said. 'I'll just be Faith, then. It's too nice a day for tears. Look, you're making Panda soggy. Let's mop you up.' But inside, her heart was breaking. It had been going so well. Too well.

To get to Thwaite Hall farm they had to drive for four miles up Yallendale along a one-track road that ran along the side of Yallendale Beck. Having recovered from her outburst, Molly was enchanted, seeing fairies in every bend of the water.

'This is lovely,' said Chris, glancing across.

'But lonely,' said Faith. 'And it can get cut off if there's a flash flood and the beck swells.'

When they got to the farm, there was no sign of Hope's car. Faith frowned, checked the time and then her mobile.

'No signal,' she said. 'The valley must be too narrow.'

A man in his thirties hurried out from the

farmhouse door. 'Dr Taylor?' he called 'I've just had a phone call from the midwife. She's been called out to a delivery, but she'd like you to do my wife's check up, please, and she'll do the home assessment another day.'

Faith got out of the car. 'That's fine. Babies come when they feel like it, don't they? Oh!' Peeping out from behind the man was girl of about seven or eight. 'I thought this was Mrs Thwaite's first pregnancy?'

'It is. Lizzie's my second wife. Alice's mum passed away three years ago, now.'

'I'm sorry.'

'Nay, we're all right. I'm Dave Thwaite, by the way.' He looked past her to the car. 'Would your man and the little lass like to come inside?'

Her man. Faith felt a small glow, followed by a pang. If only she could be sure that was true.

She introduced Chris and Molly and they went inside. Molly was charmed to have a bigger girl to play with. Chris sat down with a farming journal, all dark-haired and green-eyed and gorgeous, keeping a watchful eye on them and leaving the examination to Faith. Just for a moment as he waved her on – her breathing stopped. It was simple professional trust like that which made her determined to fight for him.

It was obvious right from the start that Lizzie Thwaite was in some discomfort. 'Sorry,' she said. 'I've had wretched back pains all night. Put the kettle on, Dave, there's a love.'

Back pain? Faith noticed Chris's head come up alertly. 'Let me see,' she said. 'You're thirty-six weeks, right?'

'Thirty-seven, now,' Lizzie pressed her hand to her back again.

'How is your general health?'

'It's fine. I was a bit worried this morning, because I seemed to have a bit of a show when I passed urine.' She hissed and moved her hand around to her front.

Faith was having a very strong feeling about this. That 'show' could easily have been Lizzie's waters breaking. And a lot of pregnant women's contractions manifested themselves as back pain in the early stages. Babies came when they felt like it all right! 'Let's get you examined,' she said. 'Where is your bedroom? And have you got a clean sheet that you don't mind getting messy?'

It wasn't even five minutes later when she leant over the banister. 'Chris,' she called. 'Can you fetch your kit out of the car too?

Mrs Thwaite is fully dilated already. We are about to deliver a baby.'

She checked pulse, blood pressure, temperature and then assessed the lie of the baby. All well. 'The baby seems to be in a bit of a hurry, but from what I can see, it should be a perfectly normal delivery. We'll have an ambulance on standby as it's premature, but both Mr Ford and I are Obs and Gynie doctors – bringing babies safely into the world is what we do.'

'Oh,' said Lizzie Thwaite faintly. 'That's good.'

The poor woman was in shock, and no wonder. One minute she was washing breakfast dishes with three weeks to go before even packing a bag for the hospital, the next minute she was propped up in bed having her first child. A little distraction technique was called for to help her relax.

Dave had already shepherded the two girls upstairs to play with baby toys in the connecting nursery – a plan they both approved of mightily. 'Your ma's on her way,' he said to his wife. 'Heaven help the local copper if he stops her for speeding.'

'Is Alice looking forward to her baby brother or sister?' asked Faith, making conversation.

'Oh yes,' said Lizzie. 'She's a lovely girl. Going to be a real little mother.'

Chris spoke, his voice diffident. 'Was it difficult at all, her accepting you?'

Faith went icy cold at the question – and was astonished to see a laughing glance pass between husband and wife!

'Lizzie's always kept the farm accounts,' said Dave, 'so Alice has known and loved her for years. We were so surprised when she burst into tears on being told Alice was going to be her new mummy.'

Lizzie chuckled. 'Turned out she thought that meant I might die, because that's what her real mother did. Funny things, kids, aren't they?'

Faith's eyes connected instantly with Chris's, seeing her own surge of hope reflected in his face. Was that it? Was that why Molly had got so upset? Because she didn't want Faith to shout and go silent and then disappear like Lorraine had done?

There was no leisure to dwell on it. The time had come for Lizzie to push. She had attended classes, had practised relaxation, she knew exactly what to do. A perfect mum-to-be. Dave supported her at every step.

Faith had been present at many births.

She had early on learnt to push aside the swell of emotion as the head appeared. It was a good thing she was concentrating. So far it had been a perfectly normal – if fast – birth. The head was nearly delivered. A couple of minutes more and ... and... No! Things weren't right. It was going badly wrong! The baby's head had appeared but was moving perhaps half an inch in and out. The face was very red. Faith knew what this was – it was called turtlenecking. If the baby wasn't delivered soon, he – or she – wouldn't make it.

Dave Thwaite was gripping his wife's hand, worry etched on his face. 'It wasn't like this with Alice...' he muttered anxiously.

Faith glanced up at Lizzie. The woman had sensed everything was not under control. 'My baby,' she gasped. 'Save my baby.'

Faith felt Chris leaning over her and drew strength from his very presence. His hand gripped her shoulder – did he know how hard? 'A shoulder distocia,' she said rapidly. 'The anterior shoulder is impacting on the symphysis pubis, and the baby can't get out.'

'First one I've seen. You've dealt with cases like this before?'

'Yes. But not many.'

'You're the physician in charge, love. I'll do what you say.'

Faith snapped into high gear, that *love* not impinging on her senses until many hours later. 'Right. Help me get Lizzie into the McRoberts position, with her knees pushed right into her chest, then you try suprapubic pressure. Rock your hand up and down on her pelvis to try and release the shoulder that's stuck. It just might work.'

It didn't. Faith stood ready to take but the body didn't emerge.

Were the baby's movements getting weaker? She ran through her options at lightning speed. She'd have to cut an episiotomy. Thank God she had her sterile scissors with her. Swiftly, she cut. Lizzie yelled, but Dave held her in a comforting grip, talking her through the pain.

Faith tuned them out. She had to. It was essential to get the baby out quickly, because with the chest compressed in the birth canal it couldn't breathe. And with a baby half in and half out, the mother's uterus couldn't contract to stop bleeding.

Now for the last imperative step. Taking a deep breath, she went to work. Carefully, using the space the episiotomy had created, she inserted her hand. Ignoring the mother's fresh wail she reached further. There! There was the forearm. If she could just apply the right pressure, just pull gently but firmly... Yes, there was movement. Faith sent up a small prayer – this baby had been so good so far, carry on that way!

The tiny body moved again. She had it! 'Push,' she shouted to Lizzie. Lizzie pushed. And the baby slipped into Faith's hands. An eyeball check and yes, the baby was breathing. 'She's alive,' she said exultantly, tears running down her face. 'Lizzie, Dave, you've got another daughter and she's lovely!'

Chris took the child from her, dried and wrapped her in the towels put ready and handed her to Dave. 'Give her to her mother,' he said.

The birth wasn't quite over. Faith pressed down on the mother's stomach. 'One more task. A last couple of pushes to get rid of the placenta, then you can cuddle your little girl.'

The placenta was delivered. Faith leaned back against Chris. 'Thank God,' she murmured and felt his arms come around her in a brief, hard squeeze. 'All okay?'

'All fine. Fabulous work. Do you want me to suture the episiotomy?'

Faith was drained. She tipped her head up

and smiled at him. 'Yes, please.'

After that it was all straightforward stuff. Faith and Chris made independent examinations of the baby and there appeared to be no ill effects of the shoulder distocia. There was the general cleaning up to be done, the bed changed, the notes to write up. A fine baby girl, weight five pounds, Apgar scale ten – the maximum.

'A lovely baby,' Faith said, and meant every word. And now that it was all over, felt a touch of envy.

There wasn't time, after all the excitement, to go on to the woodland playground. Fortunately, Molly seemed to think playing with Alice, being read to by Alice's grandma and seeing a tiny new baby was a reasonable substitute.

In some ways, thought Faith, the events of the day had bound her and Chris together even more. They'd worked as a team in the intimate atmosphere of a home birth, turning what could have been a tragedy into another small miracle of life. From the way he smiled at her when they were once more in the car, Chris thought so too. It crystallised her decision.

'I'm withdrawing my application for the

Hadrian's Wall post,' she said abruptly.

The ignition keys dropped from Chris's hand. His head swivelled to hers, his eyes green and intense. 'Really? Are you sure?'

'Yes. I'm a Dale Head and Little Allaby woman.' She felt a sense of peace that the decision had finally been made.

Chris retrieved his keys from the floor. 'I am quite ridiculously pleased,' he said, his voice muffled. 'Time to go home. Which house shall we go to, Molly? Ours or Faith's?'

Molly considered. 'Faith's for tea, then ours for bedtime,' she said, adding kindly to her father, 'Faith makes nicer teas than you do.'

Faith took a quick breath. It was too good an opening to miss and she was in an un-characteristically reckless mood. 'I make quite good breakfasts too,' she said. 'I'll have to come and stay at your house overnight some time and then I can make you one in the morning.'

She saw Chris's hands grip the steering wheel. 'That sounds nice,' he said. 'What sort of breakfasts do you make?'

'Bacon sandwiches? Eggy bread? Exploding croissants?'

'I like eggy bread,' said Molly. 'Grandma makes it.'

Faith knew. It had been the reason she mentioned it. She turned her head to look over her shoulder at the little girl. 'Shall I stay tonight and make some tomorrow, then?'

Molly smiled at her. 'Yes. And you can read me a story tonight. And Daddy can read me story too,' she added quickly.

'She's asleep,' said Chris softly. He looked across at Faith, perched on the other side of Molly's bed, and experienced a fillip of the heart he didn't remember in any of the years of his marriage. 'It's been a good day,' he said, standing up.

'Bringing new life into the world is always good.' But Faith caught her lip between her teeth as she said it.

'What is it?' Chris followed her out of the room, turning the light off.

He saw her back shrug in the dim light from the landing. 'Nothing. New life to balance old, I suppose.'

He caught up with her, drew her to him, 'Faith? You aren't making sense.'

She rested her head against his chest. If he hadn't been so concerned, he would have rather liked it, the simple trust of her in his arms. 'It was five years ago today that I

218

heard Mike had been killed,'

'Oh, Faith.' Chris held her close, feeling her pain. 'Sweetheart, tell me truthfully. Do you want to stay tonight? Or not.'

She looked up with the swift smile he had come to associate with her. 'I'd rather not be on my own tonight. I'd like to stay. But I'm going to get up way earlier than Molly tomorrow!'

Chris chuckled and bent his head to kiss her. She was soft and giving in his embrace. He kissed her eyelids, tasting tears on her lashes. He suddenly, fiercely, didn't want her to ever cry again. He would do all in his power to help her – not forget Mike, because that would be wrong – but remember him for the love they'd shared, not the sadness.

Chris moved down to kiss her lips, and as he did so he recalled what she'd said some time ago. That she'd heard of Mike's death two days before her birthday. So that meant it would be her birthday on Saturday. A day she hadn't celebrated for the past five years.

Faith was giving him back kiss for kiss, her hands roaming his back and threading into his hair. His last thought before he succumbed to the glorious passion of making love to her was that he was going to have to work pretty fast if he was going to replace her birthday sadness with beautiful memories too.

'Chris, you really don't have to do anything special,' Faith protested as he walked her down to the gate next morning so she could get ready for work.

'That's not what Molly thinks. Birthdays are to be celebrated, I'm afraid.'

'But...' She was temporarily distracted by him dropping a kiss on her hair.

'Buy yourself a new dress on the way home. That will satisfy her. See you later.'

'Yes, see you.' Faith glanced at her watch and picked up her pace. Eggy bread for breakfast was all very well, but it all took time and she was going to be late if she didn't hurry. Her feelings were all agitated. How had Molly even known it was her birthday on Saturday? Naturally she couldn't upset the little girl, but it was going to be hard to keep smiling all through that day.

She had a heavy workload that morning, but still made time for a break when she usually popped into the playroom to see Molly. Today, however, Beth Kitson paged her just as she got there to ask if she could come to the maternity unit.

'On my way,' said Faith. She glanced into

220

the playroom, but Molly was at the craft table, busy with glue and an awful lot of glitter. Faith was pleased to see she was sitting next to Hannah. Obviously she'd forgotten their little spat.

By the end of the day, shopping for clothes was the last thing Faith wanted to do. Then she got a text from Hope remarking that Chris was a fast worker and offering to meet her in town to help her choose a sexy dress.

'Over my dead body,' she texted back. She drove into town feeling manipulated.

She'd barely got home when there was an imperious knocking at the back door. It was Molly, grinning all over her face and handing her a distinctly glittery envelope.

'What's this?' said Faith.

Molly jumped up and down excitedly. 'Open it and see.'

Faith opened the envelope and brought out an even more glittery card. 'Miss Molly Ford and Mr Christopher Ford invite Dr Faith Taylor to her own birthday party down by the river on Saturday at midday,' she read. She looked up to see that Chris had followed his daughter and was leaning against the doorjamb.

'Just a birthday picnic, Faith.' There was a smile in his eyes that said he understood her reservations. 'A few sandwiches and a nice glass of wine amongst friends. All you have to do is to walk down with Molly and me and look gorgeous.'

Faith glanced ruefully at the carrier bag she'd unloaded from the boot of her car. 'I didn't exactly buy a river-bank sort of dress.'

His eyes gleamed. 'All the better.'

Faith's thirtieth birthday. She woke up to texts from her sisters and a feeling that today, whether she liked it or not, would mark a turning point between her old world and the new. Quite why, she wasn't sure, perhaps simply because she was being persuaded to celebrate, rather than regret.

Her mobile rang. Chris's voice sounded warm and velvety in her ear. 'Good morning, sweetheart. I missed you last night. Happy birthday.'

She'd missed him too, but she'd needed time alone. Things were happening a little fast. 'Thank you,' she said. 'How long have I got to make myself presentable?'

'We'll come over at eleven.' His voice became cautious. 'I believe your sisters are arriving at eleven thirty.'

She laughed. 'I can cope with them. And you're sure you don't want me to do anything? Make anything?'

'Just be beautiful. And be happy.' There was the briefest pause, as if he was on the point of saying something else, then Faith heard the thudding of small feet. Molly was evidently awake. 'Until eleven,' he said, and rang off.

Faith sat on the bed for a moment. There was something she had to do, something she'd been putting off. She pulled open the bottom drawer of her chest of drawers and took out a box holding a thick photo album. Inside the front cover was a picture of Mike smiling at her as he had done so often in life.

Just be beautiful. And be happy.

Faith looked into Mike's twinkling eyes and knew he would say exactly the same. She swallowed the lump in her throat, blew him a tiny kiss, closed the album gently and put it away.

When the time came to put on her new dress, she almost ducked out. It was surely far too frivolous for a birthday picnic by the river? She put on the slinky pink underwear from Hope, enjoying the feel of it on her skin, then slid her new purchase off the hanger. It was a silk dress in exactly that tone of pink that suited her skin. It was sleeveless, almost backless, showing just the right amount of cleavage. A summer dress.

'Some young man will think you look wonderful in this,' the shop assistant said as she carefully wrapped it. 'He'll think he's very lucky. And he'll be right.'

Looking at herself in the mirror, Faith wondered if she had chosen it with the subconscious desire that Chris would like it – and like her in it. She went downstairs thoughtfully.

'Happy birthday, Faith!' squealed Molly, bursting through the back door, dressed in her fairy party dress again. 'Daddy wouldn't let me come before – I've been waiting *ages*. This is your birthday card. I crayoned it myself. It's very nice, isn't it?'

'It's lovely,' said Faith, sitting down and opening the card.

'This is me and this is you and this is Panda,' Molly explained, leaning close to her and pointing at the people she had drawn. 'And that is me and my two friends. And those are all the fairies. And underneath it says happy birthday with love from Molly and Panda.'

'So it does! It is the loveliest card in the world and I shall put it on the mantelpiece with my other cards. Do you want to see them?'

'Not yet. You need to open Daddy's card.'

Faith looked up and there was Chris. Her breath caught in her throat. He was looking fabulous, dressed in a grey linen suit with a silk shirt in a rich green that matched the colour of his eyes. And those eyes were definitely admiring her dress!

'Hello, birthday girl,' he said and leaned down to kiss her as he put a light, rounded-oblong parcel in her lap.

Just a birthday kiss, a kiss on the cheek. But Faith felt her body respond to his warmth, his nearness, the expensive cologne he was wearing. From his indrawn breath as she turned her head to brush her lips against his, he wasn't immune to the close proximity between them either.

The sound of a car outside made him straighten up. 'That'll be my sisters,' said Faith, flustered. It was astonishing how an encounter of just a couple of seconds with Chris could send her senses straight to the bedroom and her thoughts into total disarray.

'You'd better open your nice present then,' he said, a hint of a chuckle in his voice.

'Yes, open it. It's lovely. Do you like the paper?'

Faith bent her attention to Chris's parcel.

It was wrapped in a pearlescent pale blue paper with fairies dancing across it. 'Very pretty.'

'It's my paper,' said Molly. 'Shall I help you unwrap it?'

So Molly undid the end and Faith eased out the tissue-paper inside.

'Like pass-the-parcel!' The little girl wriggled excitedly.

The parcel was soft, light... 'You've wrapped me a cloud,' said Faith with a laugh. Then the tissue paper fell free, revealing a pashmina scarf in all the pinks, purples and blues in the spectrum. She ran her fingers over it. It was so soft to the touch! And so beautiful. 'It's gorgeous,' she said simply. 'Thank you both very much.'

Then her sisters came in and the tone of the day changed to a celebration. There were hugs, kisses, more presents. Hope's was soft and squashy with a definite feel of underwiring to it. 'I think I'll open this one later,' said Faith.

Her sister grinned unrepentantly. 'Good idea. By candlelight, perhaps. After a long luxurious bubble bath.'

Which coincidentally, was what Charity's present contained. Chris looked at the contents interestedly. 'Chocolates too. And a bottle of champagne. I'm beginning to like your sisters.'

Faith wore the pashmina to walk down to the picnic. 'Don't we have to take some food?' she asked, looking at everyone's empty hands.

They all laughed at her.

It was another beautiful day, warm, with a light breeze. As they reached the bridge, Faith stopped. The normally peaceful riverbank was nearly as busy as it had been last week. 'Maybe we should find somewhere else,' she said. 'There are an awful lot of people there.'

She recognised the trestle tables from the village hall. And the bunting that appeared at every spring fete. Just as she noticed Abbey and Jack Kirk bustling around, Abbey turned and saw her. She waved madly, shouted something indecipherable, and a whole bunch of people – some of them, Faith realised belatedly, from Dale Head hospital – moved aside to reveal a banner pinned across the front of the tables.

HAPPY BIRTHDAY, FAITH!!!

Faith's hands went to her mouth in shock. The whole village was there for *her!*

'They're fond of you,' murmured Chris in her ear. 'As soon as I discussed my little idea with Abbey, she mentioned it to her friends and Jack dropped it into conversation at the Earnshaw Arms. I believe Beth Kitson and Jared Carpenter might have spread the word around the hospital grapevine too. I'm paying for the drink, but everyone else insisted on contributing the food.'

'But … but why?' Faith looked at him, bewildered.

He stroked her face. 'They've been worried, sweetheart. They respect you. They appreciate the work you've done to make Dale Head a good place. They want you to be happy.' He lifted her hand to his lips and kissed it lightly. 'And so do I.'

Molly had already gone skipping past them in her fairy dress, holding one hand of Charity and one of Hope.

'Come on,' said Chris. 'You can't run out on everyone now.'

Faith swallowed. 'I might need a hand to hold,' she said.

'You got it.'

There was an enormous cheer when Faith reached her very own birthday party. She blushed and made a hasty speech of thanks to everyone for coming – and for providing the party! More cheers, toasts were drunk, and she had small presents to open from her closest friends.

'Why?' she asked Abbey helplessly.

'Apart from to say thank you for delivering all our babies, getting me the best job in the world and keeping hospital employment local and happy?' Abbey clinked her friend's glass. 'You do ask some daft questions, Faith.'

Chris had been right. Everyone really was here because they cared about her. It made Faith feel slightly teary, but very warm and fuzzy inside. She must have been mad to think she could ever leave it and go to Hadrian's Wall. Amidst the general food, wine, beer and conversation, she felt she was living the afternoon on two levels. On one level there was a village birthday party with her sisters, friends, colleagues and neighbours. On the other level there was just her and Chris. She was aware of him the whole time, whether he was acting as host, popping the corks out of bottle after bottle of champagne, sitting next to her on a picnic rug sharing a plate of mixed savouries, or on the other side of a large group discussing rural life as opposed to urban living.

Gradually, the sandwiches, quiches, salads, tiny hot pies and bacon rolls vanished. As did the fruit skewers, the individual jellies with fresh fruit in them and the dangerously alcoholic trifle.

'Cake!' shouted Molly, and was echoed by the other children.

'I'm not sure I can,' said Faith.

'Now, now,' said Chris. 'It's a well known fact that birthday cake takes up no space at all.'

He reached down a hand to pull her to her feet. The sun had shifted, colouring his eyes a lovely deep green. 'More champagne,' he said, easing open the cork on one last bottle and pouring golden liquid into their glasses. The bubbles caught the sunlight, giving everything a magical air. At the trestle table, Jared was endeavouring to light all thirty candles on a large cake.

'I might not forgive you for that,' muttered Faith.

'Blow,' shrieked Molly.

'Yes, blow,' said her harassed subordinate. 'This breeze is getting up.'

Faith blew out all the candles, there was a cheer.

'And now you've got to shut your eyes and make a wish,' said Molly.

Faith's gaze connected with Chris. She shut her eyes and wished.

'And you mustn't tell anybody the wish or

it won't come true.'

She wasn't going to. She was hoping there would be no need.

Happy Birthday was sung, cake was distributed. Full of food and starting to get sleepy, Molly wanted to go and see Fairy Maple's tree.

'Good idea,' said Chris, putting his arm around Faith's waist.

They strolled along the path to the tree, Molly skipping a little way ahead of them. 'And then we'll go to Faith's house and then to our house,' she said.

'It would be much easier,' Chris said casually, 'if Faith came and lived with us all the time, really.'

'All the time?' Uncertainty crept into Molly's voice.

'Yes. I think it would be lovely.'

Molly pondered, the giant oak tree at her back, then turned suddenly tragic eyes on him. 'But would she stay for ever?' she said in a small voice. 'Mummy didn't stay.'

Faith hugged her, tears in her eyes, her heart melting.

'Oh, that's easy to fix,' said Chris. 'We just have to do a very special magic spell. I would have to look into Faith's eyes and say, "Dear Faith, Molly and I love you very much. Please will you marry me and live with us always?" Just like that. See?' His eyes were intense and very green and his hand hanging by his side gripped Faith's.

Molly looked at Faith and put a small hand on her leg.

Faith took it, clasping Chris's fingers with her other hand. Around them the trees rustled in the tiny breeze and the woodland scents coloured the air. Her heart filled up. She had never before known such love as she experienced right at this moment. 'Wow,' she said. 'That's powerful. And then I would have to look into Daddy's eyes and say, "Dear Chris, I love you and Molly very much too. I would very much like to marry you and live with you both always."'

'Does that mean yes?' asked Molly.

Faith smiled. 'Yes, darling. It means yes.'

'And there's one more thing,' said Chris. 'We have to seal the spell with a ring.' He let go of her hand, felt in his pocket and took out a box, murmuring, 'I've been carrying this around for *days*.'

Faith gazed mesmerised at a diamond studded circle of gold. 'Yes,' she croaked, 'that would seal the spell all right.' There seemed to be something constricting her throat. She watched as he slid the beautiful ring onto the fourth finger of her left hand. It felt warm. It felt right. She cleared her throat and tried again. 'Of course, you *could* both come and live with me instead, if you like. Or perhaps we could find a new house for all of us?'

Chris swept them both into his arms, hugging her and Molly together. 'Love you,' he said softly in her ear.

'Love you too,' she replied.

Molly sighed. 'I knew this was a magic tree.'

'It is,' said Chris, smiling at Faith. 'It really is. Magic for ever.'

Epilogue

The overnight rain had cleared to leave a softly-washed Lake District morning.

Beautiful, thought Faith, looking out of her window at the empty, peaceful hills. She was careful not to glance down the length of her garden in case Chris was also looking out of his window and they saw each other. That would never do. Not this morning. Not until roughly eleven o'clock, give or take a bride's prerogative.

Then movement caught her eye and she looked at the garden anyway. It was Molly – still in her pyjamas – scampering around the marquee in Chris's garden, through the gate and up across her lawn.

Faith ran downstairs. 'Molly – why did you...?' She stopped, because Molly was reporting to Hope, also in pyjamas, standing at the boiling kettle.

'Daddy is all waked up and he's having toast and tea with Jared. Look, he gave me some toast. And he says to tell Faith that they were very good last night and he hopes we were too. And I said we were.'

It suddenly hit Faith that she really was marrying Chris this morning. She and the girls (including Molly) had had a silly evening here with wine, chocolate and girly films. Chris – in time-honoured fashion – had been down to the Earnshaw Arms with his friends.

Hope saw her. 'Tea,' she said firmly, 'and boiled eggs and toast all round, just like you used to make for us before school.'

Faith sat down, pulled Molly up onto her lap. 'Sounds perfect. And then we'll all have showers and be ready for the hairdresser when she arrives. Then we can put on our beautiful dresses and go down to the church to knock Daddy's socks off.'

Molly laughed and wriggled round to give Faith a hug. 'I love you, Faith.'

Faith felt her heart melt. She squeezed the little girl hard. 'I love you too, poppet.'

Outside, the church bell chimed the hour. Normally, Faith barely heard it. Today, it assumed significance. The vicar, Susan Bell, had discussed the situation with them when they said they would like to get married in St Martin's church. Chris was divorced, so before she agreed, Susan had had to satisfy herself that he had done all he could to save his previous marriage, but failed. She had also seen for herself the genuine depth of attachment between Chris and Faith, and also the way Molly loved her new step-mum-to-be.

And with Molly thoroughly enjoying all the preparations of a wedding morning, it was impossible for Faith to feel apprehensive for more than just that tiny moment when she took the white silk sheath off the hanger and felt it slide fluidly down her body.

The looks on both her sisters' faces told her they had lumps in their throats.

'Oh don't,' she said. 'You'll set me off.'

Downstairs again, the flowers had arrived: shades of dark and light pink for Charity and Hope to contrast with their pink silk sheaths; a pale pink and white mixed basket for Molly to go with her first ever long pink dress; and whites and pinks for Faith to complement her colouring and her bridesmaids' outfits. The scent of roses and freesias in the cottage was overpowering!

The photographer arrived, closely followed by Faith's old consultant Freddie Myers, in splendid morning dress, who was to give her away. Her parents had sent congratulatory messages, but hadn't thought it was necessary to take time away from their work to come and see their eldest daughter married. There was just so much to do, you see. They knew she would understand.

St Martin's was only two hundred yards away. Most of the guests would walk between the church and the reception marquee in Chris's garden, but two horse-drawn open carriages stood ready at the gate for Faith, Freddie and the bridesmaids.

There were more photos, then Freddie tapped pointedly on his watch. 'Time to go. Brides can be late, but not doctors.'

The horses clip-clopped slowly down the main street. The villagers had turned out to see her, all smiling and waving. It was like her birthday picnic all over again. Faith wondered how many times that day she would be on the verge of tears.

Then they were outside the church and she was being helped down from the carriage. As Charity and Hope fiddled with her veil and arranged her train, Faith could hear organ music inside and the low murmur of the congregation.

Rev Susan Bell stood waiting in the porch in her best robes. She smiled as she greeted her.

More photos, then the vicar turned to lead the way inside. Faith took a deep breath, rested her arm on Freddie's and entered the church. The soft organ music stopped – and in its place sounded the Arrival of the Queen of Sheba. 'It's the music you deserve,' Chris had said when they'd discussed the ceremony with Susan.

As Faith walked slowly down the aisle followed by her bridesmaids, Chris turned around from his place at the front. Faith's heart almost stopped again at the sight of him dressed as splendidly as Freddie, with a white rose to match her bouquet in his buttonhole. Then he smiled at her, telling her with his eyes that he had never seen anyone as gorgeous as her, and she moved towards him as if there were only the two of them here.

Love you, he mouthed silently.

Love you too, she replied.

She barely noticed Charity take her bouquet and Hope lift her veil. All she was aware of in the whole world was the man by her side, the fluttering in her body and Rev Susan as she stood beaming before them.

'Dearly Beloved, We are gathered here...'

The publishers hope that this book has given you enjoyable reading. Large Print Books are especially designed to be as easy to see and hold as possible. If you wish a complete list of our books please ask at your local library or write directly to:

Dales Large Print Books
Magna House, Long Preston,
Skipton, North Yorkshire.
BD23 4ND

This Large Print Book, for people
who cannot read normal print,
is published under the auspices of

THE ULVERSCROFT FOUNDATION

... we hope you have enjoyed this book.
Please think for a moment about those
who have worse eyesight than you ...
and are unable to even read or enjoy
Large Print without great difficulty.

You can help them by sending a
donation, large or small, to:

**The Ulverscroft Foundation,
1, The Green, Bradgate Road,
Anstey, Leicestershire, LE7 7FU,
England.**
or request a copy of our brochure for
more details.

The Foundation will use all donations
to assist those people who are visually
impaired and need special attention
with medical research, diagnosis
and treatment.

Thank you very much for your help.